HORROR HIGH

D1600188

Final Curtain

19/01/95
H450
CJ1

Nicholas Adams

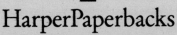

HarperPaperbacks

A Division of HarperCollinsPublishers

HarperPaperbacks *A Division of* HarperCollins*Publishers*
10 East 53rd Street, New York, N.Y. 10022

Copyright © 1991 by Daniel Weiss Associates, Inc.,
    and Sherwood Smith
Cover art copyright © 1991 by Daniel Weiss Associates,
Inc.

Produced by Daniel Weiss Associates, Inc.
33 West 17th Street, New York, New York 10011.

First printing: June 1991

Printed in the United States of America

HarperPaperbacks and colophon are trademarks of
HarperCollins*Publishers*

10 9 8 7 6 5 4 3 2

Chapter 1

When I got off the bus for my first day at Cresswell High, sleet hissed in the streets and thunder rumbled overhead. Still, I paused on the steps and looked hopefully up at the huge brick building, thinking that the worst had to be over.

After my parents got their divorce, Mom packed our things into the old Pinto and the two of us headed for New England. All the way from Arizona, she kept telling me how great it had been, growing up in her old hometown of Cresswell.

Since it was January, the farther north and east we got, the colder, wetter, and darker everything seemed. When we pulled into Cresswell at last, it was in the middle of the worst sleet-storm we'd seen yet, and the little I could see through the steamy car windows looked exactly like all the other eastern towns we'd driven through.

Mom had said brightly, "This is it, Jan! Our new home!"

Grandma and Grandpa had given us their old house, and they'd moved south where it was warm. I'd never seen the house before—they had always come to Arizona to visit. Mom drove toward where she thought the house was, but maybe she didn't remember as well as she'd thought, or maybe things had gotten built up and changed a lot. At any rate, she

1

had to stop three or four times to ask directions, and each time I heard the gas station attendant say, "But you really shouldn't go into the Lower Basin."

Guess where the house was.

When we finally reached our street, I looked out without much enthusiasm at a narrow road lined with small white clapboard houses. Old cars—like ours—were parked in front. It was real quiet as we pulled up, stopped, and got out.

"We're home," Mom said hopefully, unlocking the weatherbeaten front door.

It was stone cold inside, but the furniture was comfortable, though shabby, and the stove worked. Within a few hours Mom and I were sitting down at our table for our first meal, and making our battle plan: she'd get me registered for school the next day, then go out and look for a job.

Talking about it like that, Mom made starting a new school in the middle of a school year seem kind of like an adventure.

Unfortunately, talking and *doing* can be totally different.

It's hard to start a new school in a new city. I missed my old school so much—not that I had particularly liked the teachers, but I'd left some good friends behind. And I had known where everything was and how to get things I needed. I felt as if I'd been thrown into a maze here at Cresswell, and the game was to figure everything out all over again.

I spent my first day at school getting lost, which meant I was late to every class. In each classroom, I had to stand there while the teacher stopped talking and twenty zillion totally strange eyes scanned me. By the end of the day I felt outlined in neon, and I'd said, "Sorry, I'm lost," to so many kids, and, "Sorry, I got lost," to so many teachers, I felt like wearing a sign.

By the time I figured out which bus would get me home, I had a headache the size of New Jersey.

Mom took one look at me and said, "Was it real bad, or just medium bad?"

She looked as tired as I felt, but I knew she wanted everything to be all right, so I bit back a real answer and forced out a cheerful, "Average first day. How was the job hunt?"

Mom rolled her eyes and laughed. "I think we both deserve to go out to dinner."

The next few days weren't a whole lot better. Nothing particularly horrible happened—but I was just invisible. Hardly any of the kids paid attention to tall, skinny, brown-haired Jan Matthis, new girl from Arizona.

After a few days of walking alone, eating alone, and riding the crowded bus alone without finding anyone to talk to, Mom insisted the trick was to get into an after-school activity of some kind. I had belonged to the Drama Club back at Coville High, so I decided to go for it again.

Finding the place was the first big chore. Turned out that they didn't meet in any of the classrooms, but in the auditorium, which was this huge building on the very edge of campus near the parking lot. I fought my way across the lot against the freezing winds and squinted up at the building. It looked big and ugly and old to my eyes.

I struggled with the heavy doors and thought with regret of the brand-new, supernice theater auditorium at Coville. *That's all gone now, kiddo,* I told myself. *Make the best of it.*

The hallway inside was dark. In the huge lobby the air was as frigid as it was outside, but at least the wind was gone. The lobby had fancy stairways curving up and doubling back, and a row of big double doors leading to the auditorium itself. It had probably been a pretty nice place once—a long time ago.

Beyond the doors I heard the faint rise and fall of voices. I pushed my way into a cavernous room with a giant chandelier hanging over the middle. Thinking how nasty it would be to sit under that thing in an earthquake, I headed slowly down a side aisle toward the first three rows, where a bunch of kids were sitting. At least the auditorium itself was warm.

As I approached I gave the kids a quick scan, and my heart dropped somewhere down into my Nikes. I was pretty sure most of the kids were seniors—popular, good-looking seniors. The kind who resent the very existence of a plain junior like me. A few heads turned, looked at me, then turned away again.

I snagged a seat on the edge of the crowd, telling myself it was all in my imagination, that there had to be someone among this crowd who was an ordinary mortal. I looked around more slowly and noticed a tall bony guy with a scruffy ponytail and old jeans and a denim jacket. He wore wire-rim glasses, and though the others were ignoring him as completely as they

4

were me, he didn't seem to notice. He was slouched down in his seat, reading a battered paperback as though he were totally alone in the room.

I was just starting to relax when a blond cheerleader type in a great outfit suddenly jumped up, laughing and throwing her permed hair back in a gesture that would have made Bette Davis look timid.

When she saw me, she gave me an up-and-down look from my plain brown braid to my old jeans. Then her perfect brows wrinkled, she turned her head slightly, and in a whiny voice she said, "You know, it's about time that we got some admittance standards in this club, or we are hopeless before we begin. *Totally hopeless.*"

She sat down and an overdressed brunette stopped snapping her gum long enough to say, "Ooh, Alyssa, you are so *right.*" (*Snap! Crack!*) "Let's talk to Slater—"

I had half a mind to chuck it and bail right then. Who needed this? Then another person came in, one who stopped the talk cold.

I wish I could describe the effect Philip Devereux had. It wasn't just his looks, though he hadn't been stinted in that department. Oh, no. Tall and slim, with dark hair in a perfect cut and clothes cooler than anything you see in magazines. And it wasn't the way he moved, which wasn't slouchy or sloppy like most guys, but deliberate and even kind of elegant. He reminded me of one of those princes or dukes in the old movies, with lace at their wrists and a sword at their sides, but with lots of animal magnetism, if you know what I mean.

5

He came down the aisle toward us, smiling gently. I could feel my heart beating. This guy was so cool, he could have made ice cubes in his pockets.

Alyssa, the blonde, shrieked, "Philip! We've got a seat for you right here!"

As he continued down the aisle, his eyes scanned the rest of the room. They were unusual eyes—light blue, almost silver, with an eerie, electric stillness to them that made me shiver. He noticed me at the same moment, and his smile widened. Just a brief smile, but it was obviously for me. The first smile I'd gotten in a week at Cresswell High—and from a guy like that.

Okay, I thought, trying hard not to blush a radioactive red. *I think I can handle this school now. Definitely.*

Philip lowered himself into a beat-up seat with controlled grace, and then a second person came in late. Short and a little chubby with curly reddish hair, she rushed in, scarf flying, books about to drop from her arms, smiling widely around at everyone. Most of them acted as if she were invisible. So she probably wasn't a senior, either.

When she saw me, I made an exaggerated snooty face. She snorted a laugh and plumped into the seat next to me.

"Hi! I don't think I've seen you around before," she said. She had a high voice. "I'm Mary d'Amotti."

"Jan Matthis. I'm new in town. You, too?"

"Nope," she said cheerfully. "But I'm new to this acting stuff. Last semester I did yearbook, but it was el bore-o, so I thought I'd try something new."

Then a teacher walked in. Tall and blond, with fashionable clothes and jangling bracelets on both wrists, she clapped her hands. "Attention! It's time to choose our winter play. I see a few new faces—welcome to our drama club. I'm Ms. Slater, and I expect everyone in my productions to show up for rehearsals, on time."

She paused as a few kids laughed. "Even you, Alyssa," she said with a smile at the blonde in the front.

Several of the seniors clapped, and Alyssa fluffed her hair. She didn't look too worried.

Ms. Slater looked around at the rest of us. "Nominations are officially closed for the winter play. We are down to *The Sound of Music*, which the principal and the art students would like to see you do—"

Philip shook his head. Several kids yelled, *"Noooo!"*

"There's also the comedy *Rock and Roll High School*, which some of you indicated you'd like to do this year. And then there's *Dracula*, which is our latest nomination. You've had plenty of time to decide, so you needn't campaign now. Write your choice on a piece of paper, and pass it in."

Students started talking loudly amid the sounds of papers being ripped from notebooks. My eyes were drawn to Philip's glossy head turning this way and that as he talked to the kids clustered around him. His eyes were bright as he laughed suddenly at something one of the senior boys was saying. Alyssa giggled and fiddled with her hair. I wondered what play these guys were campaigning for.

My guess was the rock and roll one. What other choice was there, really? I wrote *Rock and Roll High School* on my paper. I'd never heard of the play, but

I'd already done *The Sound of Music* once, and I had no interest in *Dracula*—this school was coldblooded enough.

The kids quieted down when the papers were all in, and Ms. Slater read quickly through them. When she came to the last one she looked up and said, "Looks like we'll be doing *Dracula*."

Everyone burst into a big cheer.

I looked around the huge, gloomy auditorium with its spooky halls and the wind howling outside, and I thought: *Dracula? I hope this isn't some kind of omen.*

Chapter 2

"So we're going to do *Dracula*," I told my mother late that day. "Not my choice, but for some reason the other kids are really hot on it."

"It's an exciting play," Mom said. "I think you'll enjoy it. When are the tryouts?"

"Tomorrow."

"Did you meet anyone interesting in the Drama Club?"

I told her about Mary, but I was thinking about Philip. Somehow I just couldn't talk about him yet. At Coville, though I'd had plenty of friends of both sexes, I'd never had a *boyfriend*. Maybe now things would change.

The next day, I dressed with more care than usual. I figured maybe Alyssa and those other seniors at the Drama Club would be a little more friendly if I looked a little more fashionable. Also, I had to admit it—I wanted to make an impression on Philip. Maybe this time I would actually get to talk to him.

I hunted through the closet until I found one of my few skirts. It was long, slim, and black. With it I wore a maroon wool sweater and my old knee-high boots. I even changed my earrings, then smiled wryly at myself in the mirror. *You're no Garbo, kid.* But it would have to do.

After another day of being invisible through six

classes, I fought my way through winter winds to the auditorium for the Drama Club tryouts.

I arrived at the same time as Mary. She greeted me with a grin and rolled her eyes in relief. "Glad to see a normal human being here," she said, collapsing into the seat beside me. Most of her books promptly fell onto the floor.

She groaned, bending to pick them up. I helped her retrieve them, then scanned the room. I spotted Alyssa's bright head at once, in the center of a loud crowd. Several other clumps of kids sat here and there, all talking, except for that guy with the ponytail. He was slouched in a side aisle seat, reading another book. Squinting, I made out the title: *Dracula*. He seemed totally oblivious to the noise. I didn't see Philip anywhere.

A burst of laughter that came from in front of us caught my attention. A couple of boys were intent on a conversation. "So the bees killed my guy, and I only had three lives left."

"Man, that world will off you every time. Didja get the wand?"

Mary pulled a long face. "What's this? Weirdos Anonymous?" she whispered. "I mean, is this actor talk?"

"I think they're talking about a video game," I whispered back.

As I spoke, Philip came in, and a rustle of excitement went through the girls in the Drama Club. It was kind of like an invisible forest fire. Alyssa and two or three of her friends moved over to sit on either side of him. I was surprised by the strong sense of excitement that I felt seeing him again. I didn't ordinarily get big crushes on guys.

Philip said something in a low voice.

"Oh, no!" Alyssa's clone said. "I can't remember the last time someone who wasn't a senior auditioned for the play."

Next to me, Mary sighed. "What's with these people? Is that supposed to scare us?"

"Just ignore them," I advised. "They're not worth bothering over."

At that moment Alyssa looked in our direction, then away quickly. "Well, maybe this play has roles for immature youngsters." She smirked, adding, "Just as well, since we seem to have them."

Mary snorted. "I'm so upset." She rolled her eyes.

Then Philip spoke. " 'For which, they say, we spirits oft walk in death,' " he said in a soft voice that somehow managed to carry.

Alyssa giggled. "Oh, I remember that. I know what comes after. Uh . . . uh . . ." She waved her hands at her friends. "No, don't say anything, let me think!"

"Try this, then," Philip said, leaning against the back of a chair. " 'And I could a tale unfold . . .' " Everyone was silent now. He continued, " 'Whose lightest word would harrow up thy soul; freeze thy young blood—' " His voice was quiet, but oh, it was effective.

Beside me, Mary gave a little shiver. "Yucko."

"Not yucko—Shakespeare. *Hamlet*," I whispered back. "He must have done it last year." My from-afar interest in Philip increased. An adorable guy who quotes Shakespeare? Be still, my heart! Raising my

11

voice slightly, I quoted, " 'Make thy two eyes, like stars, start from their spheres—' "

Unlike the others, Philip's ears were quick. Turning to me across the heads of the other Drama Club students, he finished, " 'Thy knotted and combined locks to part, and each particular hair to stand on end—' "

"Oo-oooh," Alyssa moaned, trying to sound spooky. It got everyone's attention back on her.

Mary gave me an admiring look. "Nice going."

I shrugged, trying not to grin. "Just so happens we did *Hamlet*, too."

Ms. Slater appeared then, carrying a handful of play pages. She clapped her hands. "Time for us to begin our read-throughs. We'll warm up for fifteen minutes, then start the tryouts. Please pass these pages around."

The lights gave a flicker, and some people looked up, startled. Then there was a general uneasy laugh. The winter winds must have caused havoc with the ancient wiring in the building. The students quieted down slowly, passing back copies of the pages. I studied mine curiously; I didn't know much about the story yet. The two copies of *Dracula* at the school library had been checked out.

"Looks like Mina's the best role," Mary whispered.

I'd just come to that conclusion myself. I opened my mouth to comment just as Alyssa announced, "Toni, you'll look good as Lucy. Your dark hair next to mine—"

"Oh, I like Mina," her friend with the gum said in disappointment. "It looks like so much more fun."

Toni stopped and saw the expression on Alyssa's face. "But I'll do Lucy," she said agreeably.

"Lucy gets to turn into a vampire," a tall boy said, tugging on Toni's sleeve. He bared his teeth at her, and she squealed.

Mary turned to me, making a face. "They act like it's already settled. Yeesh! I wish I had the guts to try for a major role, but I don't know if I can memorize that much. How about you?"

"I may as well go for Mina," I whispered, fluffing out one of my skinny braids in a copy of Alyssa's favorite gesture. "My brown hair will look great next to anybody's."

Mary snorted a laugh.

The truth was, I really didn't care—then—which part I got. I just didn't like being intimidated by this girl. Maybe she was a senior, but I hadn't seen any announcement that she'd been elected Queen of Cresswell High.

"Okay now. Let's divide into pairs and warm up," Ms. Slater said.

"Want to practice?" a voice said in back of us.

Mary and I both looked up in surprise to see the guy with the ponytail and glasses addressing us. Considering how big he was, it was somewhat of a shock that he had managed to come up on us without being noticed.

"Uh," Mary said, giving him a dubious once-over.

He stared back indifferently, as though he couldn't have cared less whether we read or not. I wondered if this was just attitude, or if maybe he had also had second thoughts about the Drama Club.

"Uh, this scene only calls for two girls," Mary said.

The guy shrugged and moved away.

Mary and I read through our scene twice, switching parts the second time. I could tell she hadn't had any training—she stumbled through the words the first time, reading in a flat voice. As we went through it a second time, though, she started reading with more expression.

At the end, she looked up and said, "You know, you're really good. You make it sound easy. I really hope you'll try out for one of the leads."

I grinned, my face turning red. "Thanks," I said.

Before I could tell her about my plans to be an actress, Ms. Slater spoke.

"Boys, we'll start reading for Dracula, Harker, Dr. Seward, and Van Helsing . . ."

She paused when the lights dimmed for a long moment, then came back on. Once again there was scattered laughter. Several of the boys headed for a door in the wall next to the stage. They opened it, disappeared inside, then reappeared on the stage after a minute or two.

Following that was the usual fussing around that you get at any audition. Finally Ms. Slater moved to a row in the middle of the auditorium and called the names of the kids trying first.

One scene was about Harker's visit to Count Dracula's castle, and another was a later scene when the good guys try to trap Dracula and he fights them off. The boys who read first were okay. Not loud enough and stumbling over the words, but that's usually how it is at a first reading. Also usual was the audience whispering and rustling papers during the readings. Mary kept commenting on the guys' looks, and I realized she was seriously boy-crazy. But she was so nice, it wasn't a big pain.

As for me, there was only one who caught the Matthis eye—and he was such a class act, it'd be hard for anyone to compete. I could hardly wait to hear him read.

Philip was in the third scene, trying for the role of the Count. He almost knew his part by heart already, and he was really good—even Mary was quiet. He moved onstage with a combination of elegance and a kind of energy that reminded me of a big cat. Not a tame one, but a big one—a tiger or a panther. When he was finished, the kids burst into a storm of clapping, and Ms. Slater had to ask for quiet.

I felt sorry for the two boys who went after. They were both really self-conscious, and Alyssa laughing loudly at one who made a mistake didn't help. They came back rather sheepishly; then the guy with the glasses and another guy got up onstage.

"Frank, you take Dracula, and Paul, read Harker, please," Ms. Slater called out.

The guy with the glasses stood motionless for a minute. Then he pulled himself up straight, and his expression changed. Suddenly he sneered, and he looked *mean*.

His voice was low and husky, and when he moved, he had none of Philip's elegance, but he seemed threatening. *Menacing*. He was really good. Even the lights flickering twice somehow added to his perfor-

15

mance, rather than detracted from it: for once, no-body laughed.

His reading caught everyone by surprise. The whispers came to a stop, and kids looked up in amazement. Alyssa looked incredulous.

"What's with that guy?" I asked Mary. "Everyone looks so surprised. Is he something horrible, like a junior?"

"Tell you later," she whispered with a quick look around.

"All right, thank you, boys." Ms. Slater's voice cut through the commotion. "That was the last pair, right? We'll have some recalls later. Remember, boys, there are lots of roles besides the Count. We'll go on to the girls' roles now. It's getting late. Alyssa, why don't you and whoever else wants to read for either Mina or Lucy go on up."

"Here. Toni and I will read together," Alyssa said to her crowd. "Barbara, you can read with Heather. Come on."

"But, Alyssa, I don't really want to do a lead," a skinny blonde with very short hair said nervously.

Alyssa turned and stared at the girl. "But Heather, Barbara needs someone to read with. Come on—at least *try*."

Heather looked down and mumbled something.

I turned to Mary. "You know the way backstage?" I asked. "This place is big, and I don't want to get lost."

"Sure," she said.

We passed by Alyssa's group and headed toward the door to the stage area. I could feel Alyssa's eyes on us as we went by, and it didn't take the creaky, spooky building or the creepy story to make me imagine she was sending me what Mom used to call Bad Vibes.

It was a relief to open the door to the hallway leading backstage.

"You know, this place is kind of creepy when only the hall lights are on like that," Mary muttered.

"Kind of?" I said, glad to hear my own voice. "Huh! Compared to our theater at Coville, this place is a museum."

"A haunted museum," Mary said with a laugh.

Instead of leading directly backstage (that would make too much sense), the hallway for some reason led to a rabbit-warrenlike area behind the stage. We had to go through a couple of tiny rooms, opening doors as we went. It was almost like being in a carnival funhouse—very disorienting. And creepy.

Was that a footstep behind us? I whirled around, but no one was there. The building kept creaking as the winds outside roared, and it was too easy to think something was sneaking up on us. I shook my head. My imagination was really running away with me.

Then I heard another step—no one there. Again.

"Which way?" I asked, making sure Mary was right with me.

"To the right, I think," Mary said. "I'd forgotten they had all these closets and practice rooms—now I'm confused."

"Well, the stage should be that way," I said loudly, trying to sound cool. "Yup, up those stairs. Gosh! Those things must date back to World War II." I started up the short, steep stairs to the stage wings.

"Older!" Mary said.

Then the lights went out, leaving us in total darkness.

"Mary? You okay?" I said into the blackness. I had frozen into place, my hand gripping the banister with knuckles that I knew were white.

My heart was trying to bang its way past my ribs, but I licked my lips, thinking, *Don't panic—this is just a high school theater.*

"Mary? Where are you? The weather must have knocked out the power," I said. "Want a hand? Are you okay?"

I heard a shuffling, and I turned carefully so I wouldn't fall. I was about to start down the steps again to reach for Mary when I heard a rustle, some thumps, and Mary's voice rising in a choked, sharp scream.

Chapter 3

The lights came on a moment later.

Mary stood near the bottom of the stairs, holding on to a long, dusty curtain, trying to get her balance. She was glaring at Alyssa and two of her friends, who stood right behind her. I quickly started down toward them.

"You pushed me," Mary said, her voice shaking. "You nearly pushed me down the stairs. I could have broken my neck!"

"I tripped," Alyssa said coolly. "I grabbed what I thought was the rail, and it turned out to be you."

Mary shook her head, looking upset and furious.

"You okay, Mary?" I asked. I took Mary's arm and glared at Alyssa.

Alyssa ignored me. "Don't you have any poise?" she said to Mary in a hard voice, with a kind of weird little smile on her lips. She had a sharp face and big blue eyes. "What if the lights go out onstage? Would you go to pieces in front of a paying audience?"

"That's not fair," I said. "If the lights go off in a production, nobody will be doing any grabbing and shoving."

"I didn't shove her," Alyssa said, pushing past me and going up the stairs. "Come on, Toni, Heather. *Some* of us want to read today."

Barbara went past, giving Mary a look of sympathy,

but she said nothing. I was furious. I could feel Mary trembling slightly next to me.

"What a witch!" Mary rolled her eyes. "You'd think I tripped *her*, the way she acted."

"She did it to rattle us and make us give a lousy reading," I said.

"Just as well I'm not trying out now, then," Mary said. "It would work! Good luck," she added, rubbing her arm. "I'm going back out there before something else happens."

I ran up the steps, determined to give my very best reading.

Onstage, Alyssa gave me a cold look but otherwise ignored me. We were on the edge of the stage, next to the other two girls, who were making nervous movements toward their clothes and hair.

"We're ready anytime you are," Ms. Slater called.

Alyssa went out front with a great swirling of her high-fashion skirt, then stopped, posed, and flicked her hair back. " 'Not three proposals,' " Alyssa said loudly. Her pronunciation was clear, but her tone was flat and stagey. " 'Tell me, Lucy, about ALL of them. WHO proposed FIRST? What did you SAY to him?' " She flicked her hair again and swished around the stage while Toni read Lucy's lines about her three suitors in a high, giggly voice that made Alyssa sound good.

When they were finished, Toni walked offstage, still giggling nervously. Three people clapped loudly from the front row—Alyssa's fan club, no doubt.

"I really don't want to do this," Heather said nervously.

"Oh, Heather," Alyssa said, coming over to us.

"Who will I read with?" Barbara asked her friends. She was a short brunette with big brown eyes.

"Me," I said, stepping forward.

Alyssa shrugged and turned away, giving me a medium-cold smile. She added, "Break a leg." She didn't mean good luck. She meant major fracture.

"Nice girl," I said, then regretted it. No need for me to be witchy too.

Barbara surprised me. Her face turned a dull red, and she shrugged and said, "Oh, Alyssa doesn't mean anything. It's just that winning is real important to her. Um"—she looked away, then back at me—"mind if I read Lucy?"

I shrugged. "Either one is okay with me."

"Ready, girls?" Ms. Slater called.

We moved out onto the stage, and I took up a ladylike posture. From what I had picked up, Mina had once been Lucy's governess. Though Lucy was a noble's daughter, Mina had to work for a living. Still, the two were obviously close friends.

" 'Tell me, Lucy,' " I said, touching her shoulder. I tried for affection and confidence. " 'Who proposed first? What did you say to him?' "

Barbara clasped her hands and sighed, looking like a girl out of *Little Women.* She launched into Lucy's lines, and she was so good that I found Mina easier to get into. We bantered back and forth, both of us sounding (I thought) just like a couple of Victorian girls about to get married. I tried to make Mina older and stronger, and Barbara seemed to sense this, once

21

even sitting down and gazing up at me, like a student at her teacher.

At the end of our reading, several people applauded. Then came Ms. Slater's matter-of-fact voice, "That was Barbara Friedman and—?"

"Jan Matthis," I called into the darkness beyond the footlights.

"Thanks, girls. Sit down, please."

Even Ms. Slater's obvious noninterest couldn't douse my feeling of lighter-than-air. I knew I'd done a good reading. Nothing in the world feels as great— except turning in a good performance.

Barbara went over to her friends, who made a big deal over her. Part of Alyssa's senior clique or not, she was still a good actress.

I made my way back through the creepy maze and over to my seat next to Mary.

"You were super," she said. "Wow!"

I cast a quick look around to see if—anyone—felt the same. The big knot of Drama Club seniors blocked Philip from my view, but I was surprised when Frank with the ponytail caught my eye and made an abrupt thumbs-up gesture. Not knowing how to respond, I did the same thing back to him. He had been good too, after all.

"Students!" Ms. Slater called, clapping to get their attention. "Listen! It sounds like the weather is getting worse, so we'll meet again tomorrow at three and finish up the final readings. We'll also cast the smaller roles then."

Chair seats thundered, and kids grabbed their stuff to leave. I waited for Mary, who was struggling into two sweaters and a coat as well as a scarf. Then a hand caught my elbow.

I turned around—and looked up into Philip's face. His gray-blue eyes looked silver in this light. He was cute from a distance, but up close he was drop-dead gorgeous. I swallowed hard.

"You're great," he said. His voice was low and intimate—just the two of us. "You were real. I believed your Mina."

"Th-thanks," I managed. He smiled warmly, and my heart went into overdrive.

He turned away then, as somebody called him impatiently. I don't know how I got out of the building, but a sudden blast of Ice Age wind brought me back to earth real quick.

". . . gorgeous," Mary was saying. "And did you catch the look Alyssa gave while he was talking to you? Like an ax-murderer looking over her next victim."

"Let her." I laughed. I felt like waltzing my way to the bus stop. I could almost believe I really had a chance with Philip. *Time will tell*, I told myself gleefully.

Mary grinned. "See you tomorrow. Say! Where do you usually eat lunch?"

I shrugged, not wanting to say, "At the library, with the other invisibles."

"Well, a lot of us meet right by the cafeteria. If you feel like it, drop by."

"Okay," I said happily.

* * *

23

As we fixed dinner that night, Mom announced that she'd finally found a job as a cashier at the local supermarket, three days a week. Apparently there wasn't much work around for an ex-journalist who'd taken time out for marriage and a kid, and the little bit of money from our share of the sale of the house in Arizona was going fast.

"Great, Mom," I said, setting out the plates and silver. "I bet you'll be manager of the place in no time."

She smiled at me as she dished out our casserole. "So how was your day?"

"I read for a part in the play—*Dracula.* I think I was pretty good. I'm trying for Mina, the lead role." I didn't say anything about Philip. It was too soon and too indefinite.

"That's great, honey," Mom said. "When will you know?"

"Tomorrow." I gulped. *And with me as Mina and Philip as the Count . . . who knows where it could lead?*

"I'll keep my fingers and toes crossed—when I'm not using the cash register," she promised, breaking into my ambitious thoughts.

We both laughed, and sat down to eat.

The next day the gross northeastern weather let up a teensy bit. It was still freezing, but the sky was bright and blue. My bus was late, so when I got to school I had to run to my locker and then to homeroom, arriving just in time to get a nasty look from the teacher, and a tardy.

I realized as I left homeroom that I'd thrown my

math book into my locker with the rest of my books, and I had math first. *Great going, Matthis.*

This time my locker was jammed. I stood there yanking and grunting, and finally I lost my temper and kicked it. It sprang open. I grabbed my math book and kicked it shut again, noticing as I did a faint whiff of an odd smell. I passed Toni the Alyssa-clone a moment later, and she gave me a look and a nasty smirk that made me wonder if my shirt was on inside out.

The morning dragged, and finally it was lunchtime. I'd thought all morning about what Mary had said, and the thought of having someone to eat with cheered me up a lot as I headed for my locker.

When I pulled out my lunch bag, I noticed that weird smell again, but I shrugged it off and threaded my way down to the cafeteria.

I spotted Mary's red hair almost at once, and she saw me at the same time. She waved, and I went over and sat down.

A lot of other juniors were crowded at the table, most of them talking and eating. Mary wedged us in at a corner. It felt great to be part of a crowd again. Slowly but surely, I was starting to feel at home at Cresswell High.

"Ready for the final tryouts today?" Mary asked.

"Sure," I said.

"Me too. I rented the movie *Dracula*, and it's cool. I want to be one of the vampire ladies." She bared her teeth. "You think Philip Devereux will get the part of the Count?"

"He's got to," I said, trying not to blush at the

25

mention of his name. I looked around fast and thought I recognized the back of his head not too far away. Lowering my voice, I said, "But what's the problem with the other one who read so well? Frank, the one with the glasses."

"Oh, Frank Donnenfeld," Mary said, and looked around. "He's like at least a year older than any of us. He's doing junior year again because he missed a year by running with a rough gang. Supposedly he's stopped that now. Anyway, he spent last year in a reform school." She wrinkled her nose. "He lives over in Lower Basin—I'm sure you've heard about *that* place—and he's been arrested before. They let him out early for good behavior. So he's back here."

"Oh," I said, revising my plans to invite Mary over. I didn't blame her for her attitude toward Frank Donnenfeld—he *had* been arrested—but I gathered that my new home wasn't going to rate me any points. Not wanting to lose the first and only friend I'd managed to make, I decided to keep quiet about my address.

I was thinking about this as I started to open my lunch bag. Then I caught that weird smell again. Frowning, I unzipped the plastic bag inside the paper bag and dumped my lunch out onto the table.

Then I just stared at what used to be my sandwich, banana, and cupcake.

Mary's gasp of horror confirmed that I wasn't hallucinating.

Someone had soaked my lunch in blood, and dark rivulets were running across the table.

Chapter 4

"Eww, yucko!"

"Oh, gross!"

People at my table grabbed their stuff and backed away quickly.

"Jeez, what's that? What happened?" Mary said, picking up her notebook as a pool of blood spread toward it.

I was in shock. As I stared at my ruined lunch, I heard the distinct sound of muffled laughter—female laughter—from behind me.

I whirled around and thought I saw someone ducking through the door. Who was it? Then I looked back at my lunch, still numb with disbelief.

"Pig blood," a dispassionate voice said, as though this were no big deal. I looked up to see Frank Donnenfeld standing right behind me. "Mrs. Jackson was saying this morning that some was missing from the biology lab," he went on. "Looks like you found it."

"It found me," I said weakly. How long had he been there? Had he overheard what Mary had been telling me? "Great stunt," I said, managing a fairly low-key tone. "I'll have to remember it for Halloween." I figured whoever had done it was hanging around nearby and wanted to see me get upset. I was going to disappoint them.

"I've got enough lunch here for two," another voice, a deep, familiar, totally attractive voice, said.

I looked up, and there was Philip, carrying a tray. He set it down and gestured to the entrée.

"Oh, that's okay," I said, my face burning.

Then, out of the corner of my eye I saw Alyssa and Toni sitting down at a nearby table. "Oh, thanks, Philip," I said a little louder than I needed to. "That's really sweet of you. Just let me get rid of this mess." I got up to dump my ruined lunch in the trash and borrowed some paper towels from the cafeteria kitchen.

When I got back, I looked around, but Alyssa and her gang were gone. Frank had also disappeared. I sat down and discovered that my appetite had come back. Mary was sitting across from me, openly grinning about Philip. I kicked her gently under the table.

"When did you do *Hamlet?*" Philip asked me.

"Last year. I was Ophelia," I said. I couldn't believe we were sitting here eating lunch together. I was in heaven.

"I bet you were really good," he said.

I tried not to grin like an idiot. "You were Hamlet?"

He smiled, just a little. "Some roles are true, and easy to play."

"That's not something I ever heard said about Hamlet."

He shrugged. "Have you read much about vampires?"

"Well, not yet. It's still checked out of the library. But I plan to."

"The language is heavy going," he said. "But there's lots of better stuff that's been written since."

"That vampire junk chills me out," Mary said, cutting in. "But I love it. It's kind of sexy, the way he keeps biting women's necks."

I laughed uneasily, suddenly picturing Philip sinking his teeth into my neck while I swooned. I sat up quickly and came back to earth.

"I always research plays," I said. "My old coach told us that it was the only way to become your character, if you could live in her—or his—time and make it real for yourself."

Philip smiled at me, his eyes glinting silvery in the sunlight. He really was handsome—in a grown-man kind of way, not in a high-school-guy way. His blue button-down shirt stretched across his wide catlike shoulders, and crisp black hairs curled at the V of the collar. I swallowed hard.

"That's why you sound so real as Mina," Philip said. He stretched out his hand and just brushed it across my fingers, causing me to freeze like a statue. "You'd be perfect."

"She sure would," Mary said with enthusiasm, while I stared, hopelessly lost in the crystalline blue of Philip's eyes.

By three o'clock I was even more excited, if that was possible. Mary met me at the door of the auditorium, and we found seats together. We were among the first to get there. Alyssa and her crowd hadn't arrived yet, and neither had Philip. Frank Donnenfeld was in his usual seat toward the back, reading a book.

He never looked up as kids came in, talking and laughing.

"Did you figure out who did that to your lunch today?" Mary asked.

"Well, no mysterious notes showed up in my locker or anything," I said. "But if it was meant to scare me away from the tryouts, it backfired."

Mary grinned. "I wouldn't mind having my lunch ruined if it meant Philip Devereux would pay attention to *me*."

"What do you know about him?" I asked.

She shook her head. "Not much. He's a senior, and he's new to Cresswell. First came in September. One of my friends has a sister who's a senior, and she's talked about him. He's popular but not a socialite, and though he's dated, he's managed to avoid being anyone's steady. He's rich, and has a gorgeous car." She gave me a bright-eyed look. "And he certainly seems to like you."

"Well, he liked my reading of Mina, anyway," I said, trying to sound casual. I wasn't about to admit to Mary that I was seriously attracted to Philip—any more than I wanted to admit that this was my first attempt at a relationship.

Not that it was a relationship—yet.

Alyssa and her friends arrived then and went straight down to the front, where they started talking and joking with Ms. Slater. Several boys trickled in and dumped their books.

Suddenly Alyssa gave a shriek of laughter, tossing her hair. "Maybe the Count will get you, then," she said loudly to one of the boys. "We'll find you sitting in the senior lounge dripping blood."

Just like my bloodsoaked lunch? The unwanted memory threw me off balance. Nothing like that had ever happened at Coville High. Someone had gone to extreme lengths to make me feel unwanted. I looked around the spooky old auditorium with its flickering lights and felt a chill.

I remembered what Barbara had said about Alyssa the day before: *"She just likes to win."*

But could Alyssa have been strong enough to jimmy my locker open? That wouldn't be easy. Not for a regular person, that is; suddenly I remembered Frank Donnenfeld showing up unexpectedly. Had it been a coincidence? A guy with a habit of breaking laws would probably find lockers no big deal. . . .

I turned a little in my seat. There he was, still slouched down in his seat, one foot propped on the seat in front of him, deep in a paperback. He seemed oblivious to Alyssa and her crowd.

Not that that told me anything, I decided, straightening around again. *Get ahold of yourself, Matthis*, my brain ordered. *Time to stop the guessing games and concentrate on one thing: doing a good reading.* Because one thing was for sure—whoever had pulled that blood stunt meant for me to mess up today. I was going to show them how wrong they were.

"All right, girls," Ms. Slater called. "We'd better get started. Mina and Lucy first. We'll have second readings from Alyssa, Barbara, Toni, and Jan."

Alyssa jumped up and headed for the backstage door, followed by the other two.

I got up to join them and found that Alyssa had already arranged the reading. Toni came up to me. She was a curvy girl with heavy makeup and cold, unfriendly eyes. "We'll read together," she said in a flat voice. She gave her gum a loud snap.

I turned to Barbara, who looked uncertain. Alyssa said quickly, "Barbara and I are going to read together. Is that a problem?"

I didn't have the guts to say, "Toni's lousy—and you know it," so I just shrugged. "Fine. Let's get it over with."

"Fine," Alyssa mimicked. "You do that."

I sighed to myself. Toni gave me an icky look and started toward the stage, her gum cracking and popping at every step. So we were to go first, huh? Thanks for telling me.

Toni plunked herself down on a chair and stared stonily up at me, waiting for my first line. What a cue! But I launched into the scene, trying to block out that cold glare.

Toni read, if anything, worse than the day before. It was impossible to play off her, so I tried to shut her voice out and concentrate on my own part. Unfortunately, this was nearly impossible. I kept having a weird feeling, as if my words were sailing out into the spooky shadows of the auditorium and were being swallowed up.

At the end, I was just glad to sit down again. I knew I hadn't sounded much better than Toni. I was completely fuming at Toni's sabotage. Between this and the lunch episode, I was in a completely rotten mood.

Now I didn't stand a chance with the role of Mina— or with Philip.

Alyssa and Barbara went next. Alyssa sounded much the same as the day before, except she did more stage business. Barbara seemed nervous, and together they weren't all that more impressive than Toni and I had been.

As I scrunched down in my seat, I overheard the guy in front of me whisper, "Why do we have to go through this? Alyssa's got it even if she stands there and yodels."

The other boy, a skinny guy named Glen, snorted. "It helps if your father owns half the town and the drama coach thinks you're perfect. But I guess she wants to look like she gave the others a chance."

"Hope Slater has the brains to put Barbara or that new girl in the Lucy role," said the first boy.

"I bet she's got them all picked out—"

"Boys, now," Ms. Slater's voice interrupted from the middle row.

This time the boys' readings weren't as obviously good and bad. Philip was incredible, but so was Frank, in a totally different way. Glen wasn't too bad—he'd obviously done some practicing between yesterday and today, and a guy named William sounded pretty good, too.

When the boys were finished, they sat down, and everyone busied themselves with nervous whispers and sudden muffled laughs.

Ms. Slater smiled coolly, coming up front to stand near Alyssa and her buddies. "Well, you've all tried very hard, and I'm proud of you. It wasn't easy to choose from such dedicated students." She smiled brittlely. "After much thought, here's what I've decided for the final cast. Count Dracula: Philip Devereux."

Kids cheered and clapped, me included. I tried to meet his eyes, but he was busy smiling and looking modest.

"Frank Donnenfeld will play Van Helsing. Glen Taylor will play Harker, and William Rodriguez is Dr. Seward. For the female roles, Alyssa Perry will take Mina."

Some scattered clapping, mostly from Alyssa's friends. Even though I had tried to be realistic—it was obvious that Ms. Slater was partial to the Blond Wonder—I felt pretty disappointed. Mary patted my arm while I tried to look casual and unconcerned.

"Barbara Friedman will play Lucy. Understudies for these roles will be . . ." She called boys' names, and then mine for Mina and Toni's for Lucy.

Alyssa turned and started chattering at Philip, who didn't seem as enthusiastic—or was that just my imagination? Maybe totally cool guys never jump around like, for instance, Glen and William were doing. The thought of Philip biting Alyssa's neck made me feel sick inside.

"Now let's hear readings for the minor roles," Ms. Slater cut through the noise. "The understudies are free to try for one of these," she added, nodding at Toni.

Mary groaned. "If *you* didn't get a part, *I* never will. *You're* really good."

I tried hard to sound nonchalant. "Oh, well. There are other roles. Why not try?"

"Are you going to?" she asked.

"Sure," I said, giving myself ten points for *this* performance.

The rest of the roles were assigned quickly. Ms. Slater had us read in groups of five, then she called out the names of the winners. The seniors got the roles with the most lines. Mary was thrilled to land a part as the third vampire lady who menaces Harker at the Count's castle. The first two vampire ladies went to seniors—Alyssa's friend Heather, and another of her friends named Susan. Mary was perfectly happy with her part, though; she only had one line—a wicked laugh.

"I already know my line," she said to me, and gave a hollow-sounding chortle. "I just hope the costumes are good and creepy."

I forced a smile. I'd been given a walk-on as one of the patients in Dr. Seward's insane asylum. Gee, thanks. I knew I was a lot better than kids who'd gotten better roles, but I wasn't going to be a quitter.

"Now I can really look forward to rehearsals," Mary said, pulling on her coat and wrapping her scarf around her neck. She glanced at her watch, and her eyes widened. "Yow! My mom's waiting out there right now. I'd better hurry." She grabbed her books, then looked at me. "How do you get home? Want a ride?"

I was about to say yes, then remembered her comment about the Lower Basin. "It's okay," I said. "But thanks."

35

"Okay. Bye!" She raced up the aisle.

I followed a lot more slowly, pausing once to look back. The rest of the kids were talking, laughing, and joking back and forth—just like we'd done at Coville after auditions were over. A pang of homesickness shot through me. I thought about my old friends at Coville and how we'd pile into somebody's car after tryouts and go out to a pizza place to eat.

A closer look showed Philip right in the middle of the group. He was smiling. I could see his even white teeth from the back of the room. He didn't look up once. Had he completely forgotten about me now that I was relegated to a minor role?

I turned around and started on my way again.

When I got to the doors at the back, the cold air and the darkness seemed to close in on me. I slammed the door angrily, figuring that making noise would push the spooky feelings back. I crossed the lobby, stomping hard, then stopped at the outer doors. It was already dark. And I knew it was going to be cold.

Well, the bus ride wouldn't get over any sooner if I stood there all night. I hitched my coat closer round my neck, gripped my school stuff tighter—and jumped when I heard a step right behind me.

I whirled around to look up into Frank Donnenfeld's face. The dim overhead light flared off his glasses, hiding his eyes. He smiled slowly.

Chapter 5

"What are you doing?" I demanded, anger hiding my fear.

Frank shrugged. "I'm leaving, and this is the way out." He pointed at the door, a derisive smile on his bony face. "I thought I'd ask if you want a ride home. It might be a little chilly, but you'll get home faster."

"No, thanks," I said firmly, pushing the door open and fighting my way through the weather toward the bus stop. A little chilly? Who was he trying to kid? It would be *freezing*.

I half expected him to follow me and argue or bother me in some way, but he didn't. He didn't say anything at all—just took off slowly toward the side parking lot, where I saw a single motorcycle parked. He never even looked back.

The next day I bought a school lunch—much safer. I sat with Mary again. We'd just started eating when, lo and behold, Philip appeared. With one of those killer smiles, he handed me a brand-new copy of *Dracula*.

"What's this?" I asked, trying not to stutter.

"It's yours," he said. "See you at rehearsal."

He walked away before I had a chance to say anything.

"Wow," Mary said. "Now try to tell me he's not interested in you!"

"Don't be silly," I said calmly. "He's just excited about the play, and he remembered what I'd said about reading the book." I busied myself with slipping the book carefully into my book bag. Philip was so confusing—did he like me or not? He seemed to blow hot and cold.

When I got home, I fixed myself some hot chocolate and sat down in the warm kitchen to read the book Philip had given me. I was just getting to the Count's castle when my mother came home.

"Hi, honey," she said, looking down at the book on the table. "Homework? Oh! *Dracula*. The library finally got one of their copies back?"

I felt my face heat up. Mom looked at me with a funny sort of smile.

"Somebody gave it to me," I said.

"Oh? Does the somebody have a name?" she asked.

"Philip Devereux," I said. Just saying his name out loud embarrassed me. Trying to hide it, I picked up the book again.

"Let's see what we have to eat," Mom said, opening the cupboards.

Relieved, I carefully put my bookmark in *Dracula* and jumped up to help get supper.

Several rehearsals went by, and I threw myself into learning the play. I'd figured out in ninth grade that if you really want to do well, you don't just learn your own part, you learn everyone else's, too. And I got some chances to practice, mostly when the minor characters needed someone to warm up with or read with. Not Alyssa, though. That is, she wouldn't warm up or read scenes with anyone but Philip.

I noticed two things during those first rehearsals. Neither of them was much of a surprise. One: Alyssa may have been good looking—and she was, tall, slim, blond, and a pretty face, if a little sharp—but she was definitely not an actress. The only scenes she had a handle on were the love scenes, natch.

The second thing I noticed was that half the guys in the Drama Club had crushes on her, but she didn't even know they were alive. She pouted and flounced and yawned if Ms. Slater asked her to do anything before Philip arrived, but as soon as he cruised in the door, she made straight for him. Offstage she followed him around until he became absorbed in his work, then she'd follow him with her eyes.

He came up to me once. It was suddenly, just after I'd finished rehearsing with the others in the insane asylum scene. Everyone went back out front, but I stayed in the wings to watch. I looked up, and there he was, looking down at me. My heart leaped. "Enjoying the book?" he asked.

"Yes," I said coolly, looking away. "It's helping me see the story a lot clearer, which helps with memorizing the play—" I shut up abruptly. *What do you care if I like the book or not?* I thought. *Why don't you go ask Alyssa what she thinks?*

He didn't seem to notice. He turned and looked out over the footlights at the kids in the first rows. "That's not the first book about the immortals," he said. "But it's one of the best."

Immortals? I thought.

"I haven't had a chance to do more research—" I began, then Toni came up to us.

Giving a loud snap of her gum, she eyed me, then stepped right in front of me, next to Philip. "Alyssa wants to practice the blood-drinking scene now," she said to him. "Are you free?"

"Sure," he said, turning away with her. I almost burned with frustration. What would I have to do to keep his attention? I sighed and brushed my hair out of my face.

During the next rehearsal, when Alyssa was stumbling through her lines and stopping everyone so she could flip through her pages, I was standing in the wings practicing the lines quietly. At one point Philip was supposed to grab her when she said her line. He did, and she faltered—she obviously had no idea what to say next. So I whispered the line.

Alyssa didn't hear me, but Philip suddenly looked over her head, saw me mouthing the words, and gave me that sudden, devastating smile. Even though I had tried to resist, I felt my heart melting inside.

Other than those times, he never seemed to pay any special attention to anyone unless we were actually rehearsing; he'd sit and do his homework until it was his turn to go onstage. Once he went up there, though, he completely changed—he *was* Dracula. And the other kids would pick up his influence, everyone playing a little bit better—everyone except Alyssa.

On the day we first practiced the big scene between Mina and the Count, the one in which he tries to force her to drink his blood, Alyssa's reading was so bad that no one seemed to know what to say. It wasn't that Alyssa wasn't concentrating—she was. In fact, she was concentrating almost *too* much. She seemed lost in Philip's eyes, not that I could blame her. But every time Philip said his lines and looked at her, she just seemed to stare back, as though she had forgotten what she was doing onstage. It made the rhythm of the play totally hopeless. But Ms. Slater didn't seem to notice it.

At the end of the scene Philip dropped his pages onto a chair and ran his fingers through his dark hair. He looked pretty tired—there were dark circles under his eyes. He held out his hand to Alyssa, and she stumbled toward him. I watched his dark head bending over her bright one, and my insides squeezed.

"All right, kids," Ms. Slater called. "That was nice. Let's go over the insane asylum scene now. Quick! William, Glen, and the patients, onstage."

That was my scene. I knew it was nosy, but I couldn't help it: on my way to the stage I walked right by Philip and Alyssa. I heard him saying, ". . . and I can take you home afterward. If we meet after school all week, we'll get you caught up on your lines."

Alyssa smiled at him, leaning close. "That would be great. I don't know what's wrong with me. I seem to know my lines at home. . . ."

Thoroughly depressed, I kept going and took my place onstage. I tried not to watch them after that, without a lot of success.

* * *

The next rehearsal, the Drama Club was no longer alone.

Mary and I arrived at three to find the stage already crowded with kids. A tall, jowly teacher was talking loudly, pointing this way and that. I realized that this was the art production crew, about to get started on their set construction. From now on, we'd be working around them.

I always used to enjoy this part of a production. The kids doing crew work, or art production, would be busy building and painting sets, rarely interfering with the actors at all. In fact, it was sometimes kind of funny how actors could go on with their lines right in the midst of hammering and banging and big flats being carried back and forth. Sometimes the art production kids would stop and watch a scene, or the actors would stop and admire a newly painted flat, but in my experience at Coville the actors and the art production kids paid little attention to each other.

This time there seemed to be bad feeling between the two groups right from the start. The art production teacher, Mr. Kane, joked and laughed with his own students, but he ignored all of us—including Ms. Slater.

This went on for two or three rehearsals. I think most of us noticed Mr. Kane's attitude, particularly when he got impatient with any of us who happened to be standing around talking.

"He wanted us to do *The Sound of Music*," Mary said to me one day, while we were waiting in the wings. "I heard Glen talking to someone in English class. He'd already designed the sets and everything."

"Kane is mad because Slater never even asked him about it," William Rodriguez said, coming up behind us. "But why should she? It's *our* play. When Philip suggested *Dracula,* all of us wanted to do it. We've been doing stuff like *The Sound of Music* forever!"

"I think it's fun, but then I like scary movies too," Mary said with a smile.

"Well, now that you mention it, Alyssa's performance *is* pretty scary," I said cattily.

Mary laughed, and William rolled his eyes. I couldn't help looking for Philip, but I didn't see him. He and Alyssa came to rehearsals together every day now. And though he'd smiled at me, he hadn't spoken to me lately. I was pretty disgusted. I felt that the Alyssas of the world were always edging out the Jans of the world, with boys and play roles and everything.

"Hensen!" Mr. Kane said sharply.

A dark-haired boy started, then turned around.

"I need that flat over here. Come on, look sharp! We're going to need everyone's attention if we're to get this thing done in time."

"Try that again, girls," Ms. Slater called out from the orchestra pit in front of the stage. "Barbara, you were just right. You sound like a girl about to get married. Alyssa, we need to hear those words. Projection! Crisp pronunciation! And how about a little cheer? We have to believe you really want to marry Mr. Harker. You sound so bored with it all."

"They'll never get done." William sighed. "Come on, we may as well sit down. Our cue won't come until next week."

The boys moved off into the wings, but I stepped closer to watch the action.

"Again?" Alyssa was saying, hands on hips. "But I'll just sound more bored. This is like the sixth time we've gone over this stupid scene."

"It is beginning to sound a bit stale," Ms. Slater said, coming up to the edge of the stage and smiling coaxingly at Alyssa. "Too many run-throughs might just be counterproductive. Why don't we try Mina's first scene with the Count? We'll come back to this one later."

"Well, I guess they won't get to our vampire ladies, either," Mary said with a sigh and turned away.

Barbara came offstage in my direction. Her expression of relief made me realize that Alyssa's temper tantrums must be hard on her. Mina had a lot of scenes with the Count, but nearly every one of Lucy's scenes was with Mina alone.

I waited a moment longer. Alyssa was smiling now as Philip joined her onstage. I already knew this scene perfectly, so I decided I may as well sit down and start my math homework. I made my way back to the audience and sank into my seat next to Mary. She smiled at me sympathetically.

"Jan," a husky, low voice said right behind us.

Mary and I both jumped about a mile and a half. I whirled around to see Frank Donnenfeld standing there.

"Read this scene with me?" He pointed down at his pages, at the scene where Van Helsing and Mina figure out how to trap the Count. "I can't get her to practice." He jerked his thumb toward the stage, where Alyssa was still flirting with Philip. At least for once she was doing the scene without pages.

I was about to say no when I remembered that I was the understudy for Mina. "All right," I said. At least I'd get a chance to practice.

He shook his head. "Not here. Somewhere away from all the noise." He nodded toward the shadowy hallway offstage.

An instant sense of warning flooded through me, which I fought down. He waited for an answer, his glasses gleaming in light reflected from above so I couldn't see his eyes. Maybe the rising tension in the midst of this crazy play full of vampires was getting to me—*It's not like this guy is going to do a bloodectomy on my neck,* I thought.

"Okay," I said, trying to sound offhand.

Chapter 6

My mind went back to what Mary had said about Frank as I followed him down a half-lit, lonely hallway. I couldn't help noticing that he was big. Not fat —not fat at all—but he had broad shoulders, and his arms in the worn old denim jacket were anything but flabby. If Philip was a diamond, this guy was made out of stone.

"Uh, where are we going?" I asked.

"Band rehearsal room," he said over his shoulder as he opened a door and flicked on some lights. "Warmer than the rest because it's got no windows, and we won't hear all their noise."

"I—ah, don't want to be too far from the stage," I said hastily, trying for a normal voice. "In case they need me. Us."

Frank turned around, smiling a little as he pushed open a door I hadn't even noticed. I saw the familiar corridor leading to the backstage area. "They're just a yell away," he said.

Wondering if he was being just a tad ironic, I nodded and sat down on a large box.

"Place is riddled with rooms and halls," he went on. "The basement used to be called The Dungeon."

"How do you know how all this?" I asked.

He shrugged. "I'm doing work/study, and I landed a job in the box office," he said. "After every school concert or assembly, I help the janitorial crew sweep the place out. You learn a lot about a place, hauling trash out."

This news, though unexpected, reassured me a lot. It sounded so—well, normal. I mean, you wouldn't expect your average gang member to earn his money sweeping and dumping trash. Ex-gang member, Mary had said.

"Want to read now?" he asked.

I buried my nose in the pages that I'd brought along but didn't need; he left one door partially open, so we could hear an occasional echo of Ms. Slater's voice as she gave stage directions to the kids in the shipboard scene. I scarcely registered the low murmur of other voices.

"Where do you want to start?" I asked.

"Top of the scene, where—"

A sudden sharp voice caught our attention. A deep, man's voice—Mr. Kane. "What's going on here? Hensen, I thought I told you to get those paints back to the art lab."

To my surprise, Alyssa's voice said huffily, "I was just talking to Tom. There's no law against talking to another person who happens to be in one's class—"

Mr. Kane cut in. "You're wasting his time and mine. As it is, I don't think we'll get this play ready in time—"

A boy's voice cut in, "Okay, okay, I'm going."

"Get those paints back. And don't *you* have anything to do, young lady?"

"You're not my teacher," Alyssa said.

My eyes widened. Those were bold words, even for Alyssa.

A smooth new voice cut in: Philip. "Come on, Alyssa, time to do our scene again. Excuse me, Mr. Kane."

"All right, but remember, Alyssa Perry. You stay out of the way of my art students."

I tried not to gloat. So there was someone else besides me who wasn't impressed by Alyssa's big star attitude.

Frank snorted a laugh next to me, then said, "Anyway, let's start when Van Helsing hypnotizes Mina and she tells them where Dracula is."

"Okay. 'Professor,' " I said, the empty bandroom slowly dissolving and a cold London night taking over my imagination, " 'I have been thinking. If you were to hypnotize me now, in the hour just before dawn, then I can speak and speak freely.' "

" 'Then look up, look at my candle,' " he said.

We went on with the scene. Mina finds Dracula by a mysterious psychic connection, in the same way he's been commanding her. I tried to imagine what it would be like to be hypnotized—as if there really were a cold, dark undead power out there, waiting for me. Seeking me.

" 'Madame Mina, time is to be dreaded since he put that mark upon your throat—unless we can bring him to the death he should have earned many long years ago.' "

I fell down on the floor, closing my eyes as if I were in a real faint. My eyes opened fast, however, when I

48

heard clapping—not from Frank, but from the opposite side of the room.

I sat up and turned around.

Philip leaned in the doorway, clapping. "I'd better watch out," he said in his resonant voice. His eyes shone brightly in the glary bandroom light. It was, in fact, the most excited I'd ever seen him. "Any vampire would take you two as a death sentence," he said. "If either of you starts carving stakes, I'm out of here." He gestured toward the door, one of his hands trembling. *Faking nervousness?* I thought.

Frank snorted at the praise, but he didn't seem too put out. Me? Well, as usual when Philip talked to me, I blushed.

Philip pushed himself away from the door and stepped into the room, extending a hand to me. His thin fingers were cold, but his grip sure was strong. With a smooth, effortless movement he pulled me to my feet. "You two are great." He laughed softly. "This play will be perfect."

"Except I'm not in it," I pointed out, dusting myself off.

Philip's silvery eyes were puzzled for a moment. He looked at me, and I suddenly felt as though I were drowning in his eyes. "There's still plenty of time—" he said softly, then he froze, head at an intent angle. For a moment he stood there, still and poised, then turned and vanished. I shook my head to clear it. *What a weird effect this guy has on me,* I thought.

A few seconds later, Mr. Kane appeared in the doorway, and when he saw Frank, he frowned. "What's going on in here—Donnenfeld, isn't it?"

Frank held his empty hands a little way away from his body, as if he were about to be searched by the police. "Play rehearsal. Sir," he said, his tone respectful but his expression derisive.

Mr. Kane looked at me. Just at that moment I'd picked up my battered copy of the play. He gave a short nod, then said to me, "The rehearsals are being held in the auditorium. Stay in there."

His tone to me was much more polite than the one he'd used on Frank, though it wasn't what anyone would call *friendly*. He gave Frank another glare, then turned and left. I looked back at Frank.

"You heard the man," Frank said. He crossed the room, hit the lights, and walked out, with me trailing behind him.

Onstage, students milled around. Alyssa said in a sharp, loud voice, "Can't you art people stay out of the way for five minutes? We're *supposed* to be using this space."

"But we have to measure—" a student started heatedly.

"Hey." It was Mr. Kane, walking right out onto the stage. "My students, back to the storage area. Pronto."

He walked to the edge of the stage and peered out past the lights. "Ms. Slater," he said coldly, "your students are wandering all over backstage, in areas they don't belong."

Beside me, Frank spoke up. "We were just trying to practice where it's quiet—"

"Secondly," Mr. Kane cut through, as if no one had spoken, "your star students seem to have trouble

50

cooperating with anyone else working on this production."

"Perhaps your art students could try to keep themselves off the stage area," Ms. Slater said, coming forward. Her arms were folded, and she looked annoyed. Silence fell over all the kids in the auditorium—even though the teachers were using exaggeratedly polite voices, we all knew they were mad at each other. It was unnerving to see adults lose their tempers.

"My students are where they should be," Mr. Kane said. "If we're going to get this thing ready in time, they need to be right here. We're already behind schedule—it was my understanding that we would be doing another production, which is where most of our energies went."

"The Drama Club voted on *Dracula*," Ms. Slater said, walking up to the edge of the stage. "And we're doing our best to get it ready."

"Fine," Mr. Kane retorted, looking down at her. "So are we. But if my students can't get their work done because the stars have to be in their way, and I have to waste my time checking the halls to make sure your students aren't where they shouldn't be, then *nothing* will get done."

Alyssa chose that moment to whisper something to Toni, who smothered a laugh.

Mr. Kane gave them a look, and a vein started throbbing in his temple. His art students were absolutely still, and beyond them in the wings I saw Philip standing motionless, watching intently.

"It's no secret I preferred another play," Mr. Kane said in a hard voice. "But I was willing to cooperate. If

51

I don't get any cooperation from you, though, as far as I am concerned, this play is over. The principal might as well save time and money and cancel this thing right now. I'm ready to go tell him just that."

A burst of protests rose from all directions—even some of the art students, I noticed. But behind them, Philip stood as still as a statue. His eyes narrowed into an expression of cold hatred. I stared in surprise. What was with *him?*

"I'm sorry," Ms. Slater said. "And so are my students, I believe. We certainly don't want to cancel the play." Her meaningful tone took in Alyssa and her crowd. Heather turned red, and Toni stopped cracking her gum for once. "I think I can promise that you'll have our cooperation," she said.

"Fine. Then we'll get back to work," Mr. Kane said.

"Fine," Ms. Slater agreed.

My eyes were drawn back to Philip. I couldn't believe the expression I'd seen on his face. Had he really looked as though he were ready to kill Mr. Kane? Now Philip and a couple of art students were talking in low voices. His head was bent at a courteous angle as he listened to a short girl speak.

It must have been the lighting and the bad atmosphere in the room, I thought, relieved. *It was my imagination.*

That rehearsal ended on a down note.

As I rode the bus home, I thought it all over. For once it wasn't Alyssa and Philip that occupied all my thoughts. I thought it was unfair of Mr. Kane to take out his disappointment about the change in plays on us. Not that I blamed him for getting mad at Alyssa's rudeness, but he'd been nasty to Drama Club students before she laughed at him in front of everyone.

Now I was angry about that scene in the bandroom. We hadn't been doing anything. Maybe Frank had a bad record, but he hadn't done anything wrong —at all—during Drama Club time. Whatever else the teacher knew about him, it wasn't fair to hold his past against him if he really was trying to turn over a new leaf.

Thinking about the confrontation in the bandroom brought Philip back into my mind. What had Philip said, right before he disappeared? *"There's still plenty of time."* Did that mean he would use whatever influence he had to get me in as Mina? That was kind of exciting—except it meant getting another person out. Much as I disliked Alyssa, I felt uncomfortable about getting her tossed out of the part. She hadn't been too bad, lately—as long as Philip was there.

As the bus slowed near my street, I resolved to shove the whole thing out of my mind.

It turned out that Barbara had senior biology next door to my physiology class, last period before dismissal. If we happened to come out at the same time, she'd wave in a friendly manner, and I'd wave back. Usually Toni and the rest of Alyssa's crowd were waiting somewhere around, so of course I never went out of the way to talk to her.

A few days after Frank and I read that scene together, Barbara came out of her room struggling with her coat, books, and a big box of something that rattled. I saw her and stopped, and she said, "Give me a hand, would you?" as if we'd known each other all our lives.

I took her coat and books, leaving her the box. She gave a sigh of relief. "Specimen bottles," she said, wrinkling her nose. "To collect insects. It's not really heavy—just bulky."

"Taking it straight to rehearsal?"

"No, to my car. Is that okay?"

"Sure," I said.

"You know, you really are good in the play," Barbara said as we walked across the parking lot.

I gave her a medium-sour look. "I don't think Ms. Slater would notice me if I wore punk rock chains and leather and used a microphone onstage."

She sent me a sharp look, then dumped her box on the hood of a nice new Japanese car. "Just a sec. Let me stow this stuff." She opened the trunk, threw in all her stuff, then slammed it shut and leaned against it. Wind tore at her clothes and hair and made me shiver, but she didn't seem to notice. "You're new in town, aren't you? I don't remember seeing you around before."

I nodded.

"Ms. Slater kind of plays favorites," she said carefully. "I guess we're all used to it. Alyssa's usually decent in Ms. Slater's specialty, which is romantic stuff. Comedies."

"Somebody said that Philip talked everyone into doing *Dracula*," I said.

"Well, he didn't *talk* everyone into it, really. He just did a demo," she said, grinning. "You should have been there! It was our first meeting, last September, and Philip came for the first time. We were talking over the plays we were going to do for the year. He brought up *Dracula*, and right there he did a solo reading of one of the scenes."

"I bet he was good," I said, remembering the try-outs.

We started walking toward the auditorium. "It was incredible. Of course the girls were ready to drop the fall play, which we'd already started rehearsing, and start on *Dracula*, just because he was so cute. But even the guys got excited about it. Ms. Slater said we could vote after Christmas vacation."

"I'll bet Philip goes professional when he gets out of high school," I said.

Barbara grinned. "I think so, too. Jeez, it's almost scary, how good he is, isn't it? I think it'll be a dynamite play!"

"He wasn't exactly shorted in the looks department, either," I said, trying to be cool as we let ourselves into the auditorium's side door.

Barbara laughed. "Don't let Alyssa hear you saying that—"

She stopped talking when she saw the crowd of kids at one of the backstage stairways.

You can always tell from the way a crowd is standing if there's something wrong. William looked pale, and Glen was making a sickened face. Toni, for once, wasn't smirking and cracking gum, and I almost didn't recognize her. Barbara and I hurried down toward the crowd.

"Back up! Back up—give him room!" Ms. Slater's

voice, nervous and high, came from the center of the crowd.

The kids moved backward, and my eyes went to the drama coach and the figure she was crouching over.

"Oh, yuck," Barbara said softly.

I stared down at Mr. Kane, who lay on the floor face up, a thin trickle of blood coming from a red line across his neck. His sightless eyes stared up at the ceiling with an expression of horror that I will never forget.

Chapter 7

"You may all go home," Ms. Slater said, her voice shaking. "This rehearsal is canceled. Apparently, Mr. Kane had an accident with a hanging electrical wire. The medical authorities will be here soon, and they'll take care of him."

"Is he dead?" Glen asked. He sounded real nervous. I didn't blame him.

"No, he's still breathing. Look, it doesn't help to have you all standing around in the way. Go home. Rehearsal at three tomorrow, on time—*all* of you—and I want to see you ready to work."

Everyone moved off in twos and threes, muttering in low voices. Not a few scared looks were sent back at Mr. Kane, who was still lying there on the ground.

As I walked away, I heard the faint wail of an ambulance approaching.

"Barb? Drop me off," Alyssa said, appearing next to us. Now that I was no longer a threat, she just ignored me. She glanced back at Mr. Kane and shivered, touching the scarf around her neck nervously. "Philip had to go to the library, so I don't have a ride home."

"Sure," Barbara said. She gave me a brief smile, and they left.

I was about to turn away when my eye caught a movement in the shadows of the backstage area. I stepped forward, peering into the darkness, and recognized Frank standing by the lighting controls, staring up at some dangling wires.

My insides gave a lurch when I realized that that might have been where Mr. Kane had his accident.

Frank seemed to feel my gaze, and his eyes suddenly met mine. He turned abruptly, hiked his books under his arm, and without a word to anyone went to the door and left.

The next day Ms. Slater gathered us around her and asked for quiet. Her face was pale beneath her careful makeup. Behind her, the stage was a jumble of half-ready sets and construction equipment. No art students were in sight. The Drama Club was alone once more.

When the inevitable murmurs died away, she said, "Apparently one of the electrical wires came unstapled. Mr. Kane walked into it on his way to turn the lights on. Unfortunately, he received a bad shock and a nasty cut, but I've been assured that he will be all right."

Comments broke out—and one muffled laugh, followed by, "But Kane seems to *like* hanging around us." A boy's voice. Someone in the room didn't like Mr. Kane.

Curious, I took a quick look around at the students. Frank was slumped down in his seat, a sarcastic smile on his face. The other boys just looked blank, some exchanging whispers. Toni giggled and chomped gum, of course, and Barbara looked slightly sick. Alyssa was tense—and on her other side, Philip just sat, his expression indicating faraway thoughts. Ms. Slater raised her voice.

"Mrs. Lister will supervise the art production students while Mr. Kane recovers. As for you—and the art students will be told this as well—we want you to stay out of the corridors backstage until we've had a thorough safety check."

This caused a storm of comment, and it made me wonder what wasn't being told.

"So let's get to work," Ms. Slater said. "Act One, Scene One—we'll start right from the top."

"You people have no sensitivity," Alyssa said, getting up and looking around. "That poor man just *lying* there, and you all go on like nobody cares!" She flung out a hand in a dramatic gesture.

Ms. Slater tsked, looking helpless again.

Frank looked up. "What d'you want us to do?"

Alyssa looked sharply at him, and I wondered if she was deciding whether to actually *speak* to this disgusting creature. She must have decided it wouldn't permanently taint her (or maybe it was because nobody else made any kind of response to her surprising statement), because she said, "I think we ought to call it quits for a time, and some of us could go visit Mr. Kane in the hospital. Show some sensitivity. The art students have taken the week off from play production, and here we are, as if we don't care."

"Well, I don't," Glen muttered.

"Yeah," William said. "I mean, the guy is okay. So what good does it do him if we close up—except to put us behind?"

"He'd love that," Mary muttered. "The way he was complaining about doing this play."

Frank laughed and said, "Sounds like guilt to me."

Alyssa heard it and whirled around, hands on her hips. "What's that supposed to mean?"

Frank just shrugged, his expression sardonic. "You tell me."

Alyssa glared at him. "You think there's something sordid in visiting a teacher who somebody tried to kill?"

That got a lot of attention. A buzz of comments broke out; Ms. Slater clapped her hands, trying to get their attention again. She had no luck. Finally she yelled, "Students! There will be no irresponsible talk. Anyone who won't take my word about Mr. Kane's injuries can go talk to the principal."

Alyssa frowned. "Those of you who know anything about good manners will see that there's nothing about 'guilt' in wanting to go see him. And speaking of guilt, Frank, that's a subject *you* ought to know real well." Frank looked bored. Alyssa looked around at her usual crowd and reached for her bag. Her glance fell on Philip last. "Anybody who feels the same can come with me. Barb, you have room in your car for someone else, don't you?"

Though she was talking to Barbara, Alyssa's eyes stayed on Philip—waiting for a reaction. He said nothing.

Next to me Mary whispered, "My friend says her sister heard in the senior lounge that Alyssa is mad at Philip."

"Why?" I whispered back.

Mary grinned. "Because when they get together to rehearse, all they do is rehearse. And she has other plans on her mind."

Frank looked up at Alyssa, his glasses flashing. "I thought we were supposed to be professionals," he said. "Go on if you think it'd do anyone any good. Me, I'd rather get this rehearsal over with."

Several kids muttered their agreement.

Alyssa pointedly ignored Frank, still waiting for a reaction from Philip. Waiting for him (I realized) to do what *she* said. A battle of wills. Her gaze softened, and she looked pleadingly into his eyes.

Philip spoke quietly. "I think we should stay and rehearse. You're not taking the play seriously, Alyssa."

Another burst of whispers. Mary and I looked at each other, then back to Philip to see what he would say next.

Philip said, "I propose we all sign a get-well card for Mr. Kane. He'll appreciate that."

Ms. Slater said rather hastily, "That's a lovely suggestion, Philip. Thank you."

Philip went on, "But I agree with William—we really need the practice."

Alyssa gazed at him, her face a strange mixture of amazement and chagrin.

Next to me, Mary muttered, "She's lost him."

Philip got up and moved toward the stage. I could feel everyone wanting to stay—everyone besides Alyssa's friends. Susan and Heather got up slowly. Toni got up, whispered to Alyssa, then sat down again, unconcernedly chomping her gum.

Alyssa yanked her bag up and flounced out. Heather and Susan followed, with a lot of backward looks. Ms. Slater looked helplessly after them, obviously unsure what to do with one of her two stars walking out.

Philip turned to me, his eyes bright and steady. "Jan, will you play Mina today?"

I looked quickly at Ms. Slater, but she had no reaction.

"Sure," I said numbly.

"I knew we could count on you." He gave me that special smile, and happiness flowered inside me. I stood up awkwardly and grabbed my pages.

"This'll be good," Mary said as we walked toward the backstage entrance. "Just what you've always wanted." As we passed the place where Mr. Kane had had his accident, she grimaced. "Not that I believe anything that Alyssa says, but what was that about someone actually trying to kill Mr. Kane?"

"No idea," I said, shivering a little.

"You really want to know?" Frank said behind us.

We both whirled around. He had come up as quietly as a cat. What was it with him, always sneaking up on people?

"Sure," I said carelessly, as if I didn't really care. I didn't intend to let on that I felt off balance.

Frank pointed upward toward the dangling wire. "If it had come loose naturally, there'd be a place where it had pulled away from the wall. But that bracket was unscrewed—carefully, and on purpose. And the wire was let down just as carefully, by someone standing right about there. The only thing cut was the grounding wire." Frank's glasses flashed as he pointed toward the shadows next to the stairway. "Then someone turned the power on."

"How do you know that?" I asked.

"Looked at the wire." The end was charred and frayed.

"Yuck," Mary said. I didn't say anything.

Frank shrugged, walked by us, and up the steps onto the stage.

"Great detective work," Mary said. "I just wonder if he didn't happen to be standing around, too? Next to the stairway, maybe?"

He certainly looks capable of it, I thought to myself. I remembered the look on his face when Mr. Kane had been so snide that day in the bandroom.

But Frank wasn't the only one Mr. Kane had yelled at that day. Alyssa had a reason to be mad at Mr. Kane, too.

I thought of my bloody lunch. I was sure Alyssa had been responsible for that, just because I had been her only competition for the role of Mina. But Kane had threatened to get the play canceled. Was that enough to make her try to kill someone? I just couldn't see it. *That's why I'll never be a detective,* I thought, laughing at myself. *I just can't see anyone doing anything weird—until after it's already happened.*

As I walked up to the stage to join the others, I promised myself I would do my best not to be alone around *any* of them. Except Mary, of course.

Then I saw Barbara. She was already in character as Lucy—I could tell by the way she was standing. I

63

forced my thoughts of Frank, the wire, Alyssa, Mr. Kane, and his bleeding neck from my mind and tried to become Mina.

It was the best rehearsal we'd ever had. I know it sounds obnoxious, as if it couldn't be good unless I was reading—but it was true. Maybe it was a combination of my knowing the part compared to Alyssa's hesitations and flubs, which always seemed to break whatever mood had built up. Or maybe it was because the accident made everyone kind of serious for once.

Even Mary threw herself into her role as a vampire girl. And as for Philip—this was the first time I had ever done the part with him as the Count, and if I hadn't been so conscious of the others around me, I could have gotten hypnotized by him.

It was actually kind of eerie—while he was onstage, he *was* the Count. I found myself fighting against him as if I really were Mina—as if I had the fate of England riding on my will to resist. In the scene when he tries to force Mina to drink his blood, he stared down at me, his eyes as cold and gray as ice. His fingers dug into my arms with steely strength, and I really struggled hard, almost ripping his jacket as I tried to free myself from his grip. I really felt terrified and furious at him. I was dimly aware of utter silence in the rest of the auditorium, and when we ended the scene, me on the ground panting as if I'd run the marathon and half surprised that there wasn't blood all over my hands, I was startled when the other kids—all except Toni—clapped loud and long. It felt really good to have their praise.

At the end, Ms. Slater smiled at us. "Opening night is drawing close," she said. "You really pulled together—you're learning the real meaning of ensemble acting, just like professionals. Let's see this kind of quality from now on."

"Wow, Jan, you are so *good*," Mary said, rushing across the stage to grab me. "Oooh! I was scared to death!"

"Nice going," Glen said, swatting my shoulder with his play.

"Slater was an idiot to push you out of the lead," William muttered.

The others broke into a jumble of conversations, and I lost track of them all. I was riding high on that old, wonderful feeling that comes when you've turned in a good performance. I was part of a good team—and I knew I had done my own part well.

I floated back to the seats to get my coat and scarf and school stuff. For once, even the prospect of the long wait and bus ride didn't depress me.

"You're good," Frank said, appearing next to me, his familiar sarcastic smile in place. It made me realize that he must be used to people being sarcastic back to him.

Before I could think this through, Philip came up. He seemed to be riding the same high—his eyes blazed blue with that electric magnetism, and I couldn't look away. He took my hand in a strong grip. This time, of course, I didn't pull free.

"You made it real," he said softly, staring into my eyes. I could feel goose bumps break out on my skin.

Taking his other hand, he brushed his fingers over my neck. "You'd make a very good vampire." He smiled.

His touch made me shiver—and I laughed.

Chapter 8

When I got to school the next day, I was still feeling good from that rehearsal. I'd thought about it, lying in bed that night unable to sleep, thinking that what made acting so special was the magic that changed a play into something *real*. This "magic," hard to define, was even harder to achieve. Sometimes it happened—and sometimes it didn't. When it did, it was dynamite, ecstasy, the moon.

For the first time, I got really excited about *Dracula* itself, instead of just its male star. I wanted to make the magic happen again. Somehow, I had to play Mina for real—just once.

This feeling increased when I got to school on an icy, windy day and saw posters for the play up on all the bulletin boards. Whether or not Mr. Kane had liked the play, his art department had really gone all out; the creepy-looking, shadowy figure of Dracula even resembled Philip. I saw some knots of kids standing around looking at the posters, and later that day a couple of people in science class asked me about the play.

How they knew I was in the Drama Club, since up until then no one had even spoken to me, was a mystery—but at least I wasn't so invisible anymore.

I felt great all day.

I guess that was good, because things started going downhill at the next rehearsal.

I should have figured what was up when Alyssa came steaming in, on time—but alone. She walked down the aisle, smiling at everyone—except me, that is. Me she ignored. I wasn't just invisible to her, I was negative space. To make sure I got the message, when I went past her to sit by Mary, she backed into me, nearly knocking my books out of my arms, then went on talking to Toni as though nothing had happened. Toni almost lost her wad of gum trying not to laugh, then she hastily straightened out her face, obediently ignoring me, too.

I wondered just what Alyssa had been told about the rehearsal with me as Mina.

A moment later Ms. Slater breezed in. "I'm here, students," she said with a big smile. "And you'll all be glad to know that Mr. Kane is recovering nicely. He appreciated your note and good wishes, and he should be back with us soon." To her credit, she almost looked enthusiastic about that prospect. "Actors, in your places, please." She looked around. "Now let's see another performance like your last one!"

Glen looked dubious, several kids muttered, and Frank just snorted.

The rehearsal began, but the atmosphere this time was so much different from the last. Everyone felt serious again—but there was a lot of bad feeling in the air. However, Alyssa, who seemed to know all her lines at last, really threw herself into the role. The problem was that although she looked great and was energetic with lots of smiles and poses and hair toss ings, she just wasn't a very good actress.

It was obvious she'd decided to forgive Philip for his momentary defection, and her actions toward him onstage were kind of coy and fond. Which was exactly wrong for Mina, who was supposed to be fighting against a terrible, evil creature. Heather, Susan, and Mary all did their best to be spooky vampire ladies, and William and Glen tried really hard to match their performance of last time. Frank was always good.

But it didn't come alive.

"That was a beautiful reading, Alyssa," Ms. Slater said. "But you boys have to respond to her! Don't just stand around looking at her."

She regrouped the staging so that Alyssa was in the middle of them, and the boys all muttered and dragged their feet, but no one said anything. Philip stood in the shadows of the wings, watching.

Finally Frank walked out to the front of the stage and shook his head. "This doesn't work," he said. "This isn't a musical, with her as the big star." He jerked his thumb at Alyssa. "So why play it that way?"

"Did you spend the last year studying drama, Mr. Donnenfeld?" Ms. Slater asked, sounding tired and annoyed.

Frank threw his pages down onto a chair. His face went hard for a long moment, but then he just shrugged and sat down, his bony face expressionless.

"Unless anyone else has any more criticism to offer, let's try it again," Ms. Slater said. She moved up to the edge of the stage and stood there, frowning at the people onstage.

They went through it again, some of the kids making their resentment clear through their acting. At the end, Ms. Slater said, "Well, I can see that everyone is tired. We'll call it quits for today. I'd like you to go to sleep early and come back with professional attitudes tomorrow!"

"That sure was a bomb," Mary muttered, walking toward the seats with me. "It was so much better when you did Mina." She shrugged into her coat and grabbed her book bag. "My mom will finish the day by yelling at me for being late. Bye." She smiled briefly and started up the aisle.

"She's cute, but she can't act," Glen said, watching Alyssa laughing with her friends as though everything were fine.

"It's not all Alyssa's fault," I muttered, watching Ms. Slater pick up her briefcase and start to head out.

I was about to turn away when I saw Philip start up the aisle after Ms. Slater. He caught up with her in a few swift strides, and they went out together, the tall boy towering over the teacher.

Glen shook his head. "Alyssa is lousy. You're a thousand times better."

"Not everyone thinks so," I said, hauling my coat on.

"Huh?" William looked confused as we started slowly up the aisle.

Glen hooked his book bag over his shoulder. "I never thought I'd say this, but Donnenfeld is right. Ms. Slater just doesn't see the problem—she's directing us like we're doing some drawing-room comedy. So of course she thinks Alyssa's good."

We reached the lobby. Glen elbowed the door open and stood there while we filed out.

A screech of tires caught my attention. A little red car raced out of the parking lot. I recognized Ms. Slater's blond tangle of hair before the car zoomed away. "She must realize something's wrong," I said. "She looks mad enough now."

"Oh, she always drives like that," William said, shrugging. He grinned. "My dad almost reported her to the cops once, for cutting him off at that stop sign just before Swenson Bridge."

"Ex-CUZE me, you people are blocking the door," Toni said right behind us.

We moved hastily out of the way.

"So where shall we go for dinner?" Alyssa said brightly to her group. She looked around and saw Philip standing nearby, staring out over the parking lot. "Philip," she said coyly, and when he looked up, "how does Italian food sound to you?"

I walked away from them and headed for the bus stop. I couldn't help being resentful as Alyssa hooked Philip in yet again. I looked at her bright hair and fantastic clothes, then down at my dumpy jacket and old jeans, and sighed.

When we gathered for our next rehearsal, the art production students were busy with the sets again, this time under the direction of an older teacher. Mrs. Lister calmly went about organizing things. She paid no attention to us.

Alyssa arrived with Philip, which I tried to ignore until I saw Mary gazing at them in amazement.

"What is it? Don't tell me. Alyssa actually has a zit," I said.

Mary stifled a laugh. "No—though it would sure do her good. Jeez, how did she get him back again? I mean, after rehearsal the other day, I heard Philip trying to talk Slater into getting rid of Alyssa and giving you the part."

Despite myself, I felt my heart give a leap. "You must have heard wrong," I said, trying to be casual.

She shook her head. "I was sitting on the lobby stairway, waiting for my mom. They didn't see me, but they walked right by me. Philip was being polite and reasonable, but he was really definite. He said Alyssa'll never get the part right and that you're a natural."

"I bet that made Slater mad."

Mary nodded. "She didn't yell at him or anything, but she said quite firmly that she was the coach, and she thought Alyssa was doing an excellent job. She told Philip that Alyssa was marvelous in *The Importance of Being Earnest* last year."

Ms. Slater clapped her hands sharply right then, and we stopped talking. She explained that the design arts teacher and her students were coming to measure those of us with minor roles for our costumes.

The art students stepped forward, and for a time everything was confusion as half of us lined up for measuring. Ms. Slater decided to fill the dead time by having the leads, who had been measured a week or so ago, practice alone onstage.

While I was waiting for my turn to be measured, I stood in the wings and watched. I don't know if

Alyssa had heard that Philip wasn't pleased with her acting, or if she'd simply had what she considered a brilliant idea, but she turned up the volume on the stage business, so that every scene she had with Philip was ruined by her jaunty little twinkles and smiles.

During a pause, Frank said something to her in a low voice, and Alyssa snapped back. Ms. Slater cut in hastily, "Now Frank, Alyssa, let's try that again."

"Why?" Frank demanded, the footlights glinting off his glasses. "She's just going to keep mucking it up. This whole scene needs to be restaged."

"I think you can leave the direction to me," Ms. Slater said, an edge entering her voice.

"Yeah—I didn't know they trained drama experts in *jail*," Alyssa flashed. Toni and Susan laughed loudly.

Ms. Slater clapped hard. "Students! That's enough! I know opening night is coming soon, and we're all tense, but temper tantrums don't help."

"Jan! You're next," Mary called from behind me.

I dragged myself away from the fireworks on stage and went into the room she indicated, which turned out to be the one Frank and I had practiced in. The costume people had set up shop there.

As I stood there being measured, I could hear Alyssa's voice rising and falling sharply out front.

Thinking suddenly of Mr. Kane's accident, I felt a chill. Had somebody really tried to kill him? The idea of it made me feel slightly sick. I looked around me. Besides me and the two art students in charge of costumes, the whole backstage area was basically empty. It was creepy.

73

I heard a quiet step and looked up to see Philip at the door, his eyes concerned. "Worried?" he asked.

I shrugged, knowing how silly my thoughts would sound if I said them out loud.

He nodded toward the stage. I could hear Alyssa's giggle, then Glen and William valiantly speaking their lines. Though the words they were saying about Count Dracula were meant to be spooky, Alyssa's giggle made them sound stupid. *The real spookiness is behind the curtains*, I realized suddenly.

Then Philip spoke. "Finished reading the Stoker?"

"Days ago," I said.

He smiled, dropping down onto a partially finished stage table. "What did you think?"

"Some parts were kind of slow," I said. "Old-fashioned. But the end was exciting. I felt sorry for Lucy," I added.

Philip looked slightly grim. "The ones she loved killed her."

I was about to say, *I meant when she got turned into a vampire in the first place*, but Philip's head cocked at an intent angle suddenly. A moment later, we heard Ms. Slater's voice.

"Count Dracula. Where's the Count?"

Philip got up with his easy grace, and I got a sense again of his strength and power.

I followed him out front, and when he went onstage, I sat down to wait for my scene. Pulling out some homework, I tried to ignore how Alyssa ruined Mina, flirting with Dracula when she should have been fighting.

By the end of the rehearsal, which seemed nine

74

hours long, I had a headache—and I hadn't even been onstage. Everyone's performance was even flatter than the day before. This time Ms. Slater moved down front, and nearly every line brought new stage directions as she tried to bring the play to life.

Barbara was totally confused ("Why do you keep moving downstage, dear? Don't you realize there are two of you in this scene?"); Glen was muttering nasty insults not quite under his breath ("You're supposed to be in love with Mina—you're her fiancé. You ought to be standing behind her, giving us the impression you wish to protect her!"); William came in for his share of nastiness ("You're the keeper of the insane asylum, not a patient—let's have your talk a little less wild!"). Twice she even laid into Philip for moving away from Mina. Ms. Slater thought it had more atmosphere if they stood close together.

But the one who really got both barrels was Frank. Nothing he said or did was right, and as he and Mina had three long scenes at the end, you can bet he got a lot of flak.

Twice I thought he was about to quit and walk offstage, but he bit it back and did the scene again with just as much control as before. When he was offstage, though, the expression on his face was granite-hard. Glen and William hid out backstage during those long scenes, and I didn't even see Philip. He was there and ready when his last scenes came up, though.

The only one who handled the criticism with any kind of grace was Philip. The more Ms. Slater went on about how he could do better, the more relaxed he got, and his voice remained soft and calm. Alyssa must have thought he was actually agreeing with the coach—she clung fairly close to him, and when the order was *finally* given to break for the night, I heard her asking him where he'd like to go to dinner.

I didn't stay around to hear his reply. I'd been so sure he was interested in me when we'd started talking in the wings, my disappointment was even more painful than my feelings about the rotten rehearsal. Tears stung my eyes as I walked to the bus. What was it about Alyssa that brought him back to her every time?

Her looks, of course, and her clothes, I told myself miserably.

It didn't help that the bus took the longest it ever had to get me home; while we'd been in the auditorium, the wind had brought in an icy sleet that made cars go about a mile an hour.

When I got home, my mother took one look at me and said, "Dinner's ready. I won't ask how it went. Not like last time, I gather."

"I think I've had it," I said. "It's just not worth going back every day for the five-second walk-on part as a patient in Dr. Seward's loony bin that Ms. Slater thought I could handle. As for being understudy—I think Alyssa would show up if both her legs were broken." I told her what had happened.

My mother shook her head from time to time as I railed on about how unfair it all was. "Don't quit," she said when I'd finished. "Remember what it was like when you got your chance to do the Mina part."

"But I'm not going to get that chance again," I

said. "You should have been there today—the atmosphere was World War III. That was *without* me getting involved. If I try to assert myself with Ms. Slater, I'll be the one to get nuked. Alyssa sure won't."

Mom laughed. "You don't know that. In my experience, it's people like that who usually end up digging their own graves. But this is more important: if you plan to make acting your career, then you're going to have to get used to the Alyssas and the Ms. Slaters. The world is full of them, and they'll step on you or overlook you if they can."

I sighed. "All right, all right. I'm too tired for the pep talk."

Mom grinned. "Then I'll lay off."

I sat at the table, trying to force down the dinner I didn't want. The world seemed thoroughly lousy right then, and my plate of macaroni and cheese didn't help.

"Oh!" Mom gave a laugh. "Guess what! I forgot to tell you the big news. I got a promotion: I no longer have to work Friday nights, and I also got a raise. A small one, but enough so we can go out and buy ourselves some real winter clothes. I think we're both tired of wearing three layers of Arizona things."

I forced myself to smile back, and we talked back and forth about the grocery store, and shopping, until I'd managed to finish my dinner.

When the dishes were done, I went upstairs to do my homework. I was about four pages into my history when I heard the phone ring downstairs. From old habit my heart beat faster—but then I remembered how far I was away from home and all my old friends.

I'd just started reading again when Mom called, "Jan! For you!"

I ran downstairs, wondering if a miracle had happened and Philip had somehow gotten my number. Almost immediately I had to laugh at myself. *Just because he's got the magic for you doesn't mean you've got anything for him,* I thought, forcing my mind back to reality.

I picked up the phone. "Hello?"

"Is that you, Jan? You sound so different on the phone." It was Mary. "Why didn't I ask you for your number before? It took forever to get it from Information. I won't be able to sleep—I had to talk to someone. Have you heard what happened to Ms. Slater?"

"Who would I hear it from?" I said, just a little bitterly.

She didn't hear my tone but swept right on. "Then maybe I shouldn't tell you or you'll get creeped out, too—"

"Don't you dare say something like that and not tell me," I said, trying not to laugh. "Don't tell me she got fired—if only!"

"Oh, Jan, this is bad." Mary's voice went quiet. "She went burning rubber out of the parking lot after rehearsal today, as usual, only worse. Who knows why she was mad. Anyway, her brakes failed, and she went right off the Swenson Bridge. They just found her a little while ago. The car was almost covered by the rising water."

My mother's words flashed through my mind: *"It's people like that who usually end up digging their own graves."*

78

"Oh, my God. Is she—"

"Yes," Mary whispered. "She's dead."

"That's horrible," I said.

"Oh, but you haven't heard the worst," she went on. "This is what really creeps me out—I don't think I'll sleep a wink tonight. My brother Steve is best friends with this kid down the block whose dad is a cop. Steve got it straight from him. When the cops finally pulled her out, there was no blood in her body."

"What! What do you mean?"

"I mean that in the time between her going off the bridge and when they pulled her out a while later, someone sucked all the blood out of her body. Like a vampire." I could hear the fear in Mary's voice.

"Th-that's crazy," I said.

"You're telling me," Mary said quietly.

Chapter 9

Because of Ms. Slater's death, they canceled school for a day, and Mom and I spent part of it shopping. She was pretty shocked about Ms. Slater's accident. I just felt numb—mostly wishing Mary hadn't told me about the blood.

I almost didn't want to go back to school, ever. The news about Ms. Slater had really creeped me out. It wasn't just the blood stuff, though that was nasty enough. It was the feeling that the play was under some kind of curse. I wondered if the terrible things that had been happening were related in some way—not just the accidents to the two teachers, but the episode with my bloodsoaked lunch that day. It was all too easy to picture some crazy person lurking in the maze backstage, waiting to strike someone else. Maybe I'd be next, or Mary, or Philip.

But when I considered quitting, I remembered that wonderful rehearsal, with me playing Mina and Philip as the Count. I told myself that I was being stupid. We'd had some bad luck, that was all.

Of course, bad luck didn't explain Ms. Slater's blood being drained out—but somehow it was easier not to think about *that* at all. I mean, what would anyone do with all that blood?

The next school day was weird; the news about Ms. Slater had gotten all over. You could almost tell what kind of person someone was by his or her reaction. Some made sick faces and looked grossed out, and others—usually the boneheads—made crude remarks about vampires and bloodsuckers. Two really geeky guys showed up wearing black clothes and shades.

The thing that surprised me was how many kids in all my classes started talking about the play, and vampires in general—books they'd read, or movies they'd seen. It was as if Dracula's bloodthirst were slowly taking over the school.

Anyway, I was relieved to see a notice posted for the Drama Club rehearsal; I was afraid the school authorities would cancel the play.

When we gathered in the auditorium that afternoon, everyone was quiet.

A small, balding man came down to the front and looked us over, his bifocals gleaming. "I'm Mr. Pilson, and I usually teach freshman English, but I've taught drama before. I'll be taking Ms. Slater's place."

We looked at him expectantly as he paused and adjusted his thick glasses. Then he beamed around at us. "Several of you have petitioned the principal to continue with the play. As you pointed out, the play was one of the last projects Ms. Slater worked on, and we all believe she'd like to see it carried through. Well, I agree, which is why I volunteered to help out."

Spontaneous clapping broke out, and Mr. Pilson's cheeks turned pink.

"But you'll have to bear with me, as I get used to this again. It's—ah, been a few years." He fussed with his papers, then said, "And I'm starting, uh, in the middle of things." He smiled again. "So why don't you let me see what you have so far? Then I understand the costume people want to see the leads for a fitting."

The rehearsal, despite everyone's best efforts, was the worst we'd ever had. Every time Alyssa made a mistake, she insisted this was the way Ms. Slater would have wanted it done. Glen and William muttered unhappily—only Frank stood up to her. Philip seemed increasingly distant until, at the end of one scene, when Frank said Alyssa was so bad he couldn't finish the scene, instead of coming to her defense, as Alyssa obviously expected, Philip just stood there and looked at her, his eyes cold and unblinking. She took a look at him and burst into a flood of tears.

Sobbing loudly that Ms. Slater had been her friend, even if no one else respected her wishes, she threw herself into Philip's arms. He stood there passively under the stage lights, patted her back once, then just waited, his face absent as he stared out into the darkened seats where the audience would soon be sitting. I wondered if he expected Mr. Pilson to call the whole mess off.

Alyssa finally realized Philip wasn't melting under her charm. I watched them, my heart in my throat. Did I have a chance with Philip after all? Alyssa looked up at Philip with tear-drenched eyes, then pulled herself together. "I'm all right," she said tightly. "Let's go on."

"Why? She's never going to be any better. We're dead in the water," Glen muttered as he tugged at the tight collar of his costume. The play was rapidly turning into a nightmare—a jinxed nightmare.

It took Mr. Pilson three more scenes, then he called for an end. With obvious relief everyone trooped off-stage, some of them going for costume fittings. Even the art production kids seemed subdued, though Mr. Kane was due back on Monday.

Mary was one of the ones called for a fitting, so I packed my stuff alone and started up the aisle toward the exit.

I was surprised when I heard a step behind me, and Philip stood there. "Jan, some of us feel we still need to practice, so we're going to have a rehearsal at my place later on. Can you make it?"

"Yes," I said, delighted. Then I remembered the small matter of transportation. "But where do you live? I don't know if the bus—"

"Glen knows where I live," he said. "Is it all right if he picks you up? He said he'd be glad to."

"Uh, never mind," I said quickly. "I'll just take the bus." With my luck, Frank Donnenfeld and I were the only ones in the whole school who were stuck in terrible Lower Basin.

Glen ran up the aisle just then. "I just called my brother on the pay phone, and I can borrow his car. What's your address?"

"It's too much trouble," I said. "I'll find out which bus—"

"Actually, I live pretty far from the nearest bus stop," Philip said. "Is there a problem with Glen giving you a ride?"

Both boys stared at me, waiting for an answer.

"No," I said, flushing hotly. "Here, I'll write it down for you." I dropped my books on the floor and ripped out a sheet of notebook paper. I wrote my address hastily and folded the paper over. Glen shoved it into his pocket.

Philip looked from one of us to the other, and smiled. "I'll see you around six."

Glen showed up an hour after I got home. In that time I'd been able to take a shower, put on brand-new jeans and my nicest sweater, and explain to my mother that this was *not* a date, it was a rehearsal. Not that she would be able to tell from my flushed face, pounding heart, and clammy palms.

Mom was totally cool when Glen arrived, which was lucky. Glen was obviously nervous and didn't want to come inside. He stood right next to the front door and kept looking out at his car as if he expected it to disappear—or, I realized with a sinking feeling, as if he expected some lowlife to come along and trash it any second.

"I'm ready whenever you are," I said as soon as he finished the polite small-talk with Mom.

Glen was obviously relieved. His expression when he looked at me was different in a way I couldn't immediately identify.

"Bye, kids. Drive carefully," Mom said.

"Sure, Mrs. Matthis," Glen said. His expression said, *Out of this area as fast as I can,* and I realized what his expression had meant: he'd been reassessing me.

"Sorry about the address," I said calmly as we got into the car.

Glen blushed—I saw it even in the dim light. "Uh, it's okay, I mean—it's not your fault—"

"This neighborhood was okay when my mother

grew up here," I said. "I guess my grandparents didn't notice it had suddenly become Trashville."

Glen winced. "Hey, look, Jan. It's no big deal."

But it was—I'd seen it in his face. It made me really mad. Still, I knew that chewing him out about it wasn't the way to make friends at Cresswell High.

"Right, no big deal," I said, biting down my anger. "So what do you think of the play?"

With this safe topic cooling the hot air between us, he visibly relaxed. We talked about how horrible it was about Ms. Slater, and how weird it was she hadn't noticed her brakes going bad, and so forth. We didn't mention the blood. Glen got us to Philip's as fast as he could, and I was glad.

Philip lived with his uncle, Glen told me as we drove up a long, tree-lined street toward a big old house. He added to what Mary had told me: Philip had come in September from another state, Vermont, he thought. One of Philip's parents had been killed in a skiing accident, and he'd come to live in Cresswell. Glen didn't know where the other parent was.

Philip's uncle answered the door, and it was apparent from his greeting that Philip's Old World–type courtesy was a family trademark. He reminded me of one of those British actors who also has a noble title: very refined. He led us down a wide hallway lined with paintings and busts on pedestals. At the end of the hall, he threw open wide double doors and announced that this was the "salon." We found most of the rest of the cast sitting with polite nervousness on the edges of chairs that belonged in some kind of a museum. The artwork on the walls was also museum-quality stuff, not to mention the crystal in the chandeliers and the porcelain vases, but when Mr. Devereux wished us a good evening and retired upstairs, he didn't say, "Be careful." Heck, if my mother had seen the place, she would have warned us to Watch It Or Else. If it had been my house, I would have sweated buckets every time someone swung an arm. Not Philip.

As soon as his uncle went upstairs with his leisurely tread, he said, "Now we can start."

"Won't it, uh—bother him if we get a bit loud?" Glen looked even more nervous than he had when he saw where I lived.

Philip shrugged slightly. "His rooms are at the back of the house, and his hearing isn't all that great. Don't worry. Shall we get started? Let's have this half of the room be downstage." He gestured toward the curtained French windows.

"What about Frank?" William asked. "Is he coming?"

"He called just a while ago. He won't be able to make it," Philip said. "So I thought we could try the scenes without Van Helsing tonight and see how it works."

Heather and Susan glanced at each other. "What about Alyssa?" Heather said with a quick glare in my direction. "She's the most important person."

Philip smiled at her. "Jan will do Mina tonight. Alyssa needed a rest. Come on, you can help us out, can't you?" He held out a hand to Heather, looking calmly into her eyes.

Heather looked at him, hesitated, then sat down

86

with a confused expression on her face. From behind her, Barbara rolled her eyes at me, and Mary grinned.

"Act One, Scene One," Barbara said, standing up and clapping her hands.

We did the play right up until Lucy is turned into a vampire, just before Dr. Seward calls Van Helsing in to help. It really went very well. Philip served as the director, making his suggestions in a mild, low-key way. Each suggestion he made bettered the scene, and even Heather and Susan sometimes forgot about being Alyssa-clones and got into the spirit of the play.

It was strange, acting it out there in that old-fashioned house, like something out of London at the turn of the century. Being in that setting made it easier to pretend that I was Mina. The magic started stirring . . . and it almost went *real* again. Almost.

The only times I got thrown out of it were when Heather or Susan caught themselves and gave me those piercing glares. I had a pretty good idea that Alyssa hadn't even been invited to this rehearsal, and I knew who would be burning up the phone lines to report on this evening's rehearsal as soon as they got home.

And Philip wouldn't get the flak for it. I would.

When we got to the end of the first act, Philip brought out some coffee and soft drinks. After a little talk, in the smoothest way possible, he got Heather and Susan out the door.

The rest of us stayed, and Philip suggested we try just a few scenes from Act Two. This time it was even better, very smooth and natural. When it was clear we couldn't go on without Van Helsing, everyone was disappointed.

As Mary and the others reluctantly started going for coats and gloves, Philip said something to Glen, who shot a quick look at me. Before I had much time to wonder what it was about, Philip came over to me. "Can you stay for just a little while? I'd like to try some of Mina's scenes with the Count. I'll drive you home afterward."

"Sure," I said, feeling really strange. Was this it? Was Philip going to make his move? Would we be a couple by tomorrow?

I sat on the edge of an embroidered chair and tried to look interested in a leather-bound copy of Keats's poetry that I found on an elegant table, as Philip saw everyone to the front door.

When he came back into the salon and shut the door, the sudden silence was loud.

I stood up nervously. "Uh, Philip, I've been thinking. Isn't this kind of a waste of time?" I asked. "I mean, there's no way Alyssa will give up the part. She sure won't take any suggestions from me."

"Wouldn't you like to play Mina?" Philip said.

"Well, sure, but—" Philip came closer to me and took both my hands in his. His hands were smooth, strong, and warm. I felt infinitely safe. Looking into his eyes, I felt my reservations slipping away.

"Let's try it." He turned away, moving toward the other side of the room.

I felt both relieved and disappointed that he really did want to practice the play. *So much for his interest in*

Jan Matthis, future star, I said to myself. Of course, the evening wasn't over yet.

Then I didn't have time to think anything else, for he spoke his lines, and I responded—and this time the magic took over fast. I really *was* Mina in the flesh, and I was alone with a vampire.

We both knew the play so well that it was as if the others were still around in ghost form, saying their lines. We spoke to them and heard their answers, but the real action, the focus of the play, was between Philip and me as the Count and Mina. A delicious tension built steadily between us, moving swiftly toward the inevitable confrontation. Fear prickled down my spine as Philip strode toward me.

" 'You dare to cross my will,' " he snarled, grabbing me by the wrists. His fingers dug in, and I wrenched free of his grip.

" 'Begone, demon,' " I gasped. " 'I will never submit!' "

" 'You will be mine,' " he said, with a horrible laugh. His eyes widened, bright as twin lasers. " 'Now and forever.' "

And swift as lightning, he grabbed me again. His grip was hard. Fear electrified me—I was really fighting for my life against the king of vampires. I struggled with all my strength to break free, scarcely noticing a flash of silver on the edge of my vision.

"Taste my blood and join the Immortals!" he breathed into my hair—and with a tremendous effort I wrenched free, lost my balance, and landed hard on the floor. The spell was broken.

I sat up slowly, shaking my head, then froze when I

caught sight of a smear of blood on my wrist. Looking up, I saw that Philip really had cut himself—I was startled to see a knife in his hand. *Where did that come from?* I stared at it, rubbing my arm, which ached where I had wrenched away from his grip.

Awareness of the here-and-now came back slowly. I looked down at my hands, noticing that my wrists were rapidly turning pink and purple with bruises. I felt *scared*. Philip just stood there staring at me, breathing hard. He was so still, and tall—taller than normal, it seemed, and that smile of his was no longer gentle and kind, it was . . . waiting. *Sinister.*

For a few seconds I wondered if he was really going to attack me—what had I gotten myself into? What was happening? Then we heard a light tap on the door. Philip started, then froze.

Philip's uncle appeared and flicked on a light. "Oh, still at it?" he inquired in a mild voice.

Philip's head turned fast, the hall light outlining one of his high, taut cheekbones. Then he spoke. "We just finished, Uncle Charles," he said politely, calmly. He came toward me and the light fell on him again. I saw that the knife had disappeared. He extended a hand to pull me up. I got shakily to my feet. Mr. Devereux nodded, smiled vaguely, then said good night. I responded in a choked voice, and he withdrew. Alone again, I couldn't quite meet Philip's gaze.

"I'll get your coat. It's later than I thought." His voice sounded completely normal.

What's wrong with me? I thought, shaking my head. I hadn't allowed a scary movie to get to me since I was twelve, and here I was freaking out over a *play*.

90

Maybe it was the aftermath of Ms. Slater's death—and Mr. Kane's accident. Those things were certainly scary when I stopped to think about them.

But . . . I looked up at Philip doubtfully. For a moment, the play hadn't been a play at all. It had almost felt like Philip had really wanted to hurt me. But that was nonsense. Everyone knew that Philip was nice and always polite. I had been imagining things.

I breathed deeply, trying to shake the mood, as Philip reappeared with our coats and his keys. We walked to the front door, and he held it open for me; then we went out into the icy winter air.

His car was like the house: elegant and old-fashioned, a sleek black sports car. As I slid into it, I smelled something unfamiliar but *expensive*—a real leather interior. The engine started up at once and stayed quiet as Philip drove with smooth, controlled speed out into the wind-scoured street.

"I wish Frank had been there tonight," I said, trying for normal conversation. "His Van Helsing is so good. Why didn't he come?"

Philip said, "Frank called from the police station."

A cold hand seemed to grip my insides. "Why?"

"He said they wanted to ask him some questions about Ms. Slater's car. Somebody had tampered with the brakes." Philip's voice was soft and remote, as if this were happening to people long ago in an unreal place.

"You don't think he did it?" I asked cautiously.

Philip looked over at me again, a quick smile. "No. Do you?"

I shrugged. "I don't know—I didn't even know

about the business with her brakes! That's horrible. I mean, I'm not sure I liked her, but I don't think she deserved—all *that*." I didn't even want to ask about the drained blood.

" 'A fitting tribute,' " he said, with a distant smile. "A line from the play. Did you know we'll have a full moon on the night of the dress rehearsal?"

Glad to get off the subject of Ms. Slater's accident, I said, "No, I didn't. Well, maybe its magic will help us." *We'll need it.*

"The night the vampires walk abroad," he said. "Do you think they'll come see us?"

I grinned at the wind-tossed trees flashing by Philip's car. Here was someone else who understood about the magic, the drama becoming real. Entering into the game, I said, "Do you think they'll believe in *us*?"

Philip pulled up suddenly at a red light and leaned over to touch my hand. "With you as Mina, it will be real," he said.

"Yeah, well, tell that to Alyssa," I said, remembering suddenly that the part wasn't mine. "Here—two streets more, and my house is sixth down."

Philip's Jaguar swept around the corner and moved quietly down my street. Philip parked in front of the house and got out, not looking back at his car or at the street. I smiled inwardly. I knew he was special. His eyes were on me as we walked to the door. "Good night, Mina," he said with a courtly bow.

"Good night, Count," I said, executing a curtsey as gracefully as I could in my jeans and hightops.

"Have faith—you'll see," he said, stepping down

onto the sidewalk. The wind blew his dark hair across his eyes so I couldn't see his expression. His soft voice was all but obliterated by the creaking trees, but I still heard him. "We can't disappoint the Immortals," he said, and laughed.

Chapter 10

I stepped out of the snow-frosted bus on Monday, and my eyes lit on one of the *Dracula* posters. I grinned at it, thinking not only about the play but about the fast ride in Philip's car as we had joked about vampires.

Does he take his magic to the play, or does it come with the play and settle around him in the real world, like Dracula's velvet cloak?

Whichever it was, the memory of that rehearsal at his house was potent stuff. If we could just get that same power working in the play onstage, it would be a performance to remember.

Imagining the glowing words a Broadway director would be speaking on our opening night after he discovered us, I started slogging my way through the dirty slush toward the school building.

Before I'd gotten far, a boy, a big football-type whom I recognized from my math class, called, "Hey, Jan!"

"Yeah, Marc?"

"Aren't you in this vampire thing?" He jerked his thumb at the poster.

I shrugged. "A little part only."

"Hey, cool!"

Some other boys laughed.

"Isn't he the guy playing the neck-biter?" Marc asked, pointing into the student parking lot.

I turned around and saw Philip, tall and slim in a really handsome overcoat, standing near a red car. He was talking to someone, and from the angle of his head, I could tell he was very intent on the conversation.

I craned my neck and saw Alyssa's familiar blond head. She looked up into Philip's face, and though the gently falling snow between me and them diffused their expressions, I could see that she didn't seem too happy.

I nodded at the guys. "That's him—Count Dracula in the flesh."

They laughed, and one guy grabbed his neck and started making noises as if he were dying. I started on my way again, with a couple of backward looks at Philip and Alyssa.

What were they talking about? I saw Toni join them, her jaw working furiously. She yelled something at Philip and grabbed Alyssa by the arm and they both walked away, leaving Philip standing there watching after them.

I forgot about my wet feet slowly going numb in the slush as I peered through the thickening snow, trying to see Philip's face. Alyssa knew about Friday night. I wondered what Philip had told her.

"So what happened?"

The deep voice behind me made me jump. I whirled around, ready to annihilate whoever had sneaked up on me—and I looked up into Frank Donnenfeld's face. As usual, he had taken me by surprise.

My anger must have been obvious, for his old deri- sive smile twisted his lips. "You've convicted me with- out a trial, too, huh?" he said, and started to move on past.

I didn't think—I just shoved my hand out and caught hold of his denim-covered arm. Somewhat to my surprise, he stopped. "What are you talking about?" I said.

"You don't know about my Friday-night fun at the slammer?"

"You're getting blamed for Ms. Slater, is that it?" I said.

Staring up at Frank with his scruffy ponytail and his old denim jacket, I realized I was *not* convicting him without a trial. That is, I no longer thought of him as Trouble, despite the gossip about him that I'd heard. He'd always been perfectly nice to me. All of a sudden I saw Glen's snap judgment about where I lived in a new way; I'd done the same thing to Frank.

He shrugged, the derision back in full force. "Obvi- ous choice, right?"

I sighed. "Look. I try not to accuse people of any- thing without evidence."

"Then you're a minority of one," he said. His tone was still derisive, but his eyes were no longer hostile. He was reassessing me, too. "All the evidence this crowd needs is the wrong address." He shrugged one of his broad shoulders in the direction of Toni's candy-apple red car.

"If that address is in the Lower Basin, they'll have to arrest me too," I said, and laughed at the surprise in Frank's eyes. "You should have seen Glen's face when he drove up to my place on Friday! I think the morgue has more class, in his opinion."

Frank's eyes narrowed, then he abruptly dropped the attitude. "So what happened at Philip's rehearsal without Alyssa?"

"We were hot," I said. "Which only creates more problems."

He glanced at his watch, then started walking. I fell in step beside him.

"Do you think they really were accidents?" I asked.

Frank squinted down at me. "You know who Kane was ragging on that day? Before he bounced us out of the bandroom, I mean?"

"Alyssa," I said, thinking back.

Frank nodded. "Right."

My jaw dropped, and I stopped dead in my tracks. "You *don't* think *she*—"

Frank said, "I can see her trying to strangle Kane— or anyone else who gets in her way. Can't you?"

"I don't know," I said uncomfortably.

"She's spoiled rotten, and she doesn't think other people are real."

"But what about Ms. Slater? She thought Alyssa was great!"

Frank hesitated, about to say something, then he just shrugged. "If someone else meets with an accident, then maybe my guess will be right."

"Someone else like who?" I asked.

"Like you," he replied.

I drew a deep breath. "Then you do think it's Alyssa?"

97

"Let's see what happens," he said, and added with a narrow look, "You watch your back."

He walked off abruptly, leaving me standing there alone in the snow. The bell rang then, making me alone, cold, and *late*.

"No rehearsal?" Mom said when I got home.

"Now that Mr. Kane is back, the art department needs the whole stage, and the lighting people are practicing, so Mr. Pilson gave us a day off."

"Is there a problem with the play?" she asked, looking closely at me.

I'd been thinking about what Frank had said. It was bad enough worrying that the play was somehow jinxed, but to think that Alyssa—or someone—had caused those accidents on purpose? It was too awful to believe. But someone *had* definitely, deliberately, drained all the blood out of Ms. Slater.

At lunch, Mary had told me that Heather had been talking about quitting the play entirely. She was really afraid that the play was cursed, but everyone had pressured her to stay.

They were there Friday night. They felt the magic, too.

"Well?" Mom asked.

I looked up and shrugged. One thing was for sure; I wasn't about to tell Mom about Frank's suspicions. Cool as she was, I knew what she would say. "Sorry, I was thinking about something else," I said lamely.

"Would that something else be somebody named Philip Devereux?" She grinned at me.

"Mom!"

"I'm not nosing, I'm not nosing," she said, raising her hands.

"There's nothing to nose into," I admitted modestly.

"You like him, but he's not interested?"

"He is—I think. Sometimes," I said, thinking of our conversation in the car on the way home.

"I'd like to meet him," Mom said casually.

"Wait until you see him onstage," I said.

Barbara met me at the door of my science class the next day. "Did you know that Philip tried to talk Alyssa into quitting yesterday?"

"I saw them in the parking lot, but I didn't know what was going on."

"Well, Toni called him eighteen kinds of slime mold for it, then went around trying to get everybody to agree to kick *you* out of the play, as if this were all your idea." She winced. "She even tried to get the art kids into it and ended up having a big fight in the senior lounge with one of the art students, a guy named Tom Hensen, who thinks you would have been picked in the first place except for the old Slater nepotism. You can imagine how everyone loved that."

"Wow," I said, feeling strange. "But I haven't done anything wrong. I'm not going to let their stupidity force me out. I won't quit. If it turns out Alyssa doesn't play Mina, then I will."

Barbara gave me a quick smile. "Good. Time for rehearsal."

We walked across the snowy lot toward the auditorium. As I walked, I remembered what Frank had said, and I made a resolution to keep an eye on Alyssa. Frank's prediction that I would be the next victim was both scary and confusing.

When we got inside, the tension was measurable on the Richter scale. Toni took one look at us and flounced off to Alyssa's side. Heather and Susan were there as well, and most of the other kids sat on the opposite side of the room. It was kind of like two armed camps.

Great, I thought. *The Trojans against the Greeks. Only I don't make much of a Helen of Troy.*

Mr. Pilson was there, looking nervous and uncertain. He was making announcements about fittings. Some people had their costumes already and wore them onstage, which gave the scene a weird look—modern jeans and cool shoes mixed with dark suits and long dresses.

Philip smiled at me when I came in but otherwise did not come my way. I felt kind of bad and kind of relieved. I stayed well away from Alyssa, hoping she didn't have any hanging wires in her purse.

The rehearsal started right away. At first I tried to stay in the wings, but this was easier to plan than to do. The art students didn't appreciate having someone in their way, and Mr. Kane, who was back for his first day, finally said to me, "Can't you look for somewhere else to loiter?"

I took one look at his thundercloud brow and the purple scar on his neck, and I changed my plans.

I rejoined Mary in the front, watching the action onstage. This time Alyssa played her part loud and angry. It was slightly better than Mina as the town flirt. Nobody said anything at all to her, including Mr. Pilson.

When it was my turn to go onstage, I went around to the back, away from Heather and Susan. Toni was nowhere in sight.

The rest of the insane asylum patients piled on the stage and we took up our positions. I could see from their faces that despite the tension, or maybe because of it, they were out to have some fun.

The idea was for us to act crazy in the background while Dr. Seward and Harker interviewed the patient that Dracula was using mind control on. One boy was rolling around on the ground like a snake, and a couple of girls acted as if they were covered with bugs. I sat on a ragged bed and made faces and clawed at anyone who came near me.

This time we all really put ourselves into it. After the tension of the day, it felt good to lie there and moan artistically. I think some of the others picked up on the feeling, because there were more hisses and animal noises than ever. In front of us, the boys playing Harker and Dr. Seward gave us a pained look and raised their voices.

"Good!" Mr. Pilson called. "Much better!"

Harker and Dr. Seward sharpened up their focus, putting lots of energy into keeping us in the background. I felt the scene coming alive around us—

Then through all the noise came a horrific scream.

My first thought was, *Somebody is really overdoing it.* Then I heard Mr. Kane shout, "Hey! Stop!"

The kids onstage faltered and fell silent. Near the wings I saw Frank, waiting in his Van Helsing frock coat and boots, turn quickly to stare into the darkness backstage.

People started moving in that direction—I got up and followed, my heart banging. Around me I heard worried mutters: "What's wrong?" "What happened?"

We fell silent when we found Toni lying on the floor in a heap. Mr. Kane was kneeling by her, trying to lift her up. She wheezed for breath, her hand to her throat.

Mr. Pilson pushed his way through the crowd. "What's this?" he said, his voice high and sharp. "Someone trip? You art students shouldn't leave your equipment lying around for anyone to—"

His voice trailed off when Toni fainted. Her head rolled back, and we all saw the purple bruises around her neck.

Chapter 11

"I heard noises," Mr. Kane said. "The light was off, so I came back here to investigate. I didn't see anything, but I heard what sounded like a struggle, then a girl cried out, so I yelled *stop*, and then I heard running steps. When I found the lights and turned them on, this student was lying here."

"Who wasn't onstage?" Mr. Pilson demanded of us. All four of the leads raised their hands. Frank leaned against a wall with his arms crossed, looking sardonic as Mr. Kane and several others turned first to stare at him.

Heather and Susan also raised their hands. I saw Alyssa scan the rest of us, her eyes falling last on me. I wondered if she'd been about to blame me for attacking Toni—but she couldn't, since I'd been right in the middle of the stage.

Mr. Pilson gazed at Barbara, Alyssa, Frank, and Philip as if they'd grown extra arms. I felt sorry for him—he obviously didn't know what to do next. Barbara looked as if she were going to throw up, and she sat down abruptly. Mr. Pilson watched her, then rubbed his head, which was gleaming with sweat. "You were all standing in the wings?" he asked.

The kids looked at each other and shrugged.

Mr. Pilson turned to Mr. Kane and said, "Can you account for all your art students?"

"I'm about to find out," Mr. Kane said grimly. "Art production! Down front, pronto! The police will be here in a few minutes, and I for one will be damned glad to see someone go out of here in cuffs." He fingered the healing scars on his neck.

Mr. Pilson looked helplessly around at us, then said, "It could have been someone who gained access to the building who doesn't belong with either my actors or your crew."

"We'll find out," Mr. Kane said. "I promise you that."

They herded us all out to the seats, where we stayed while the police and paramedics swarmed in. Toni was rushed off to the hospital, and while the sirens wailed away in the distance, every one of us was questioned by a detective.

Those of us who'd been onstage were dismissed right away. The detective kept the other actors, then Mr. Pilson kicked out those of us who'd been dismissed.

The last thing I heard was Alyssa's voice, rising in angry protest, that she had been in the wings, and anyway, Toni was her best friend.

"Mr. Pilson and Mr. Kane want to cancel the play," Mary said on the phone a little while later. She'd called almost as soon as I walked in the door.

"Why? Did the police catch anybody?"

"That's just it—they didn't. They can't prove it was any of us or not, and they're acting as if the play is under a curse or something."

I heard her words with mixed feelings. It no longer

seemed possible that Alyssa was responsible for the attack; I realized I had actually started believing that she was the troublemaker.

But she wouldn't attack her own friend. Who could it be, then? "What happened after I left?" I asked. "Why did they keep you with Frank and Philip and Alyssa?"

"Because no one could vouch for having seen me."

"How come?"

"Well, that's what I wanted to tell you. See, I followed Toni backstage. This was while you were up onstage, in the crazy scene. I was sitting a few seats behind Alyssa and Toni, then Toni said that she was going to the rest room. I just got a funny feeling, so I decided what the heck, if she really went to the rest room, I needed to go too. So anyway, she didn't even go near it. She went back to the room where the art people keep their stuff."

"Really? Did you tell the cops all this?"

"You kidding? Who knows what they'd blame me for! All I told them was that I went to the rest room, which was true. And since I didn't do anything to her, I don't feel bad about leaving out the rest."

"So what was Toni doing?"

"I don't know. I couldn't exactly stand there in the doorway and watch her, so I left and went to the rest room anyway. But I just *bet* she was going to do something nasty to somebody. Remember the pig blood? I bet that was Toni's idea. Alyssa wanted you scared, and Toni seems the type to think of ways to do it."

"Yuck," I said.

"So anyway, when I came out, the light in the hall

was off, which was weird. Then I heard Toni scream, and I just panicked and ran like crazy in the other direction!"

"I don't blame you. I would have done the same thing. When I was leaving, it sounded like they were trying to blame Alyssa, but that's silly."

"Yeah. I don't think anyone seriously thinks Alyssa would hurt her best friend. Then Mr. Pilson sent us all home, and he said he'd post a notice about further rehearsals, which doesn't sound too good."

"Great. All that work down the drain."

"Well, Alyssa threw a fit. I left then—she was yelling at poor Pilson at the top of her lungs about all her hard work—and Ms. Slater's death—going for nothing. She was a real witch. I felt sorry for the guy."

"That'll probably ruin any chance of the play happening," I said.

"Yes," she said, and sighed again. "Well, see you at school."

I got off the phone and started upstairs.

"What was all that about?" my mother called after me. "Not that I mean to spy, but a mother's ears do tune in fast when her daughter mentions the police."

I took a seat in the warm kitchen, and while my mother fried up some tacos for dinner, I told her about Toni's strangling—leaving out the stuff about Toni trying to get me thrown out of the play. Mom kept shaking her head, but she didn't say anything until I was finished.

"It must have been some punk," she said at the end. "But just the same, if that building is half as big and drafty and dark as you say, I'd think twice about going anywhere alone in it. In fact, I wonder if maybe you should just give this one up. You'd said you weren't really thrilled about *Dracula*, anyway."

"Oh, Mom," I groaned. "Nothing will happen to me—anyway, it'll probably end up getting canceled."

Mom shook her head, but before she could speak, the phone rang again.

"Good grief, Grand Central," she said, smiling at me.

I had to laugh. Nowadays it was a miracle if the phone rang twice in one week. Mom used to say that about Grand Central when it rang every five minutes.

I picked it up, thinking it had to be for Mom, so when I heard a soft voice say, "Jan?" my heart nearly dropped through my shoes.

"Philip? Oh, you're not calling to say the play's canceled, are you?"

"No, no. I'm calling to tell you the play *hasn't* been canceled. I think I've talked them out of it."

I sighed with relief. "Did they figure out who attacked Toni?"

"*They* think they have," he said.

"Well, at least we won't have to worry about any more people getting jumped," I said.

He laughed softly. "I don't think you were ever in any danger."

"Oh, I don't know," I said, remembering what Mary had said about Toni.

"What do you mean?"

"Oh, just Toni's mouthing off," I said, feeling uncomfortable gossiping about a girl who'd just gone to the hospital after being nearly strangled. "Though I don't think she's the violent type—just pulls mean tricks. You know, like the blood in my lunch."

"Yes, Alyssa told me today that it had been Toni's idea," Philip said.

"Well, anyway, I'm glad the play is still on."

"That's why I called," he said. "I wondered if you'd come help me run through some of the crucial scenes. I'd like to reblock them."

I was about to say, "What about Alyssa?" but I didn't. I wanted to go with him—and I wanted to play Mina, even if it was just once more.

"Sure," I said.

My mother had no problem with my going off to a practice, as long as I wasn't going alone, so Philip said he'd be by in twenty minutes to get me. This gave me fifteen minutes to brush my hair and change my clothes.

Philip was right on time. I grabbed my coat, yelled "Bye!" to Mom, and ran outside to meet him. The icy wind swirled around me, making me shiver.

Philip got out of the car and came around swiftly to open the door for me. *What a gentleman.* I slid gratefully onto the warm seat. The door shut on the storm, closing me into a safe little world. Some kind of classical music was playing on his CD deck, something with a piano running up and down the scales in a compelling melody.

He got in on his side and smiled at me. I smiled back, feeling suddenly how *close* he was. His eyes were wide and silvery, and he radiated energy. This was our second time alone together.

"Ready?" Philip asked, his strong hand moving fast on the gearshift.

I nodded, and reaching for some kind of balance in an atmosphere that seemed too intense for such a small space, I said, "Uh, what music is that?"

"Chopin," he said. "Don't you like piano?"

Without waiting for an answer he flicked off the CD, and with one hand almost carelessly controlling the steering wheel, he put another CD in. Fretful, tense music drifted out—one instrument, then another, then another.

"Shostakovich," he said. "Eleventh Symphony."

"It's kind of weird—different, I mean."

"The theme is revolution," he said, sending me one of those bright-eyed smiles.

"Definitely not boring," I said with a slightly nervous laugh. "But I didn't think the other one was, either. I just don't know too much about classical music."

"I think I spent half my childhood being dragged from one European concert hall to another," he said. "But at least I know what's good."

The music built in intensity as he drove uptown at a headlong pace. The wind occasionally rocked the racing Jaguar, but otherwise the weather stayed at bay. I realized at one point that I hadn't even asked where we would be doing this rehearsal—but just when I was going to frame the question, I recognized the road.

We turned down the long street toward school, flashed over the Swenson Bridge, and pulled into the empty parking lot, stopping in front of the auditorium.

I broke the long silence then. "Can we get in?"

"I got a key from one of the teachers."

"How'd you manage *that?*" I asked, thinking it odd.

"It's easy enough if you know how to ask," Philip replied.

It probably helps a lot if you are handsome and charming and kind and polite. I let the subject drop.

He unlocked the big front door and led the way in.

The lobby seemed as icy as the air outside, and I pulled my coat closer around me. Philip sailed through the dark lobby, his long overcoat swinging behind him, and pulled the doors to the auditorium open.

I followed more slowly, groping my way in the dark. The theater seemed impossibly large, and the winds scouring over the top of the building made mysterious rustlings in the thick shadows. I wished Philip hadn't gone so far ahead. It was too easy to imagine a hand darting out to grab at me, and I tried to stumble faster down toward the orchestra pit.

By the time I made it to the first rows, Philip had already found the stage lights and flicked them on. I felt reassured at once by the familiar sight of the mostly finished stage setting for the Count's castle.

Philip ran backstage, then appeared onstage and reached down to pull me up, too. "You don't need pages, do you?" he said.

"Nope." I shivered in my coat, moving my arms back and forth. "You grew up in Europe? That must have been fun!"

" '*Le sort fait les parents, le choix fait les amis,*' " he said, smiling wistfully. With a fast, impatient movement, he shrugged out of his overcoat and slung it across the back of a chair. Part of it flopped down so the expensive silk lining spilled onto the dusty stage.

"If that's a quote, I don't recognize it," I said, reaching down to straighten his coat so it didn't get dirty. "My French is about as good as a three-year-old's. Something about parents—you didn't, what, choose your parents, so . . ."

"But you choose your friends. Jacques Delille," he said, frowning slightly as he stared at the ground. He stood there in his white shirt and dark slacks, and he didn't seem to notice the cold. "Ready?"

I gave up trying to ease into the play. "Sure."

"Act Two, Scene Four."

"Right. I'm over here," I said, moving to the back. "You've just scared Van Helsing and the rest away."

Philip smiled again, showing the edges of his strong white teeth—and suddenly he was Count Dracula.

Halfway through the fourth scene I had warmed up, and my grungy old coat flopped onto the floor beside the chair holding his elegant one. We played two of the scenes over again, Philip switching in and out of character so fast, it was startling. When he was himself, it was to look around with a preoccupied frown.

It was exciting, even exhilarating to be alone with him, working on the play. At first I wondered when we'd stop and just start talking—like any girl and guy —but after a while his mood affected me and I forgot about everything but the play.

We completely restaged three of Mina's scenes with

the Count. Though they played much better, I wondered briefly if Mr. Pilson would be upset—these were scenes that Ms. Slater had wanted done a certain way.

But there wasn't time to think—we were too busy. Philip was intensely focused, almost in a hurry, as if there was some kind of invisible deadline he had to meet.

I asked about it once. We'd rehearsed so long, my feet were getting tired and my mouth was dry. Abruptly realizing that I was pooped, I leaned against the plywood fireplace and watched Philip drag two pieces of prop furniture to a different position.

"Isn't this good enough for now?" I asked. "I mean, Mr. Pilson's going to have something to say about all this restaging—"

Philip looked over at me and blinked, as if he had forgotten I was there. "It has to be right," he said. "It has to be perfect."

His voice was exactly as soft as always, but something about his tone was utterly convincing. Of course the play had to be just right—I was an actress, wasn't I?

So we tried it again, and this time we finished the scene.

When we had gone all the way through it, Philip looked at his watch and exclaimed, "It's nearly midnight. Will you get into trouble?"

"No. We had lots of late rehearsals at Coville. It's just that I've never had a late one with only one other person before."

He didn't get the hint, and I began to understand,

even sympathize, with Alyssa's frustration. "Let's get you home."

Philip slung his coat over his shoulder and gestured toward the back of the auditorium. "Go on up to the lobby, and I'll turn out the lights."

I jumped down from the stage and ran toward the entrance, feeling almost lightheaded with tiredness and exhilaration.

The weather had cleared, leaving the icy streets gleaming coldly under the light of brilliant stars. The world seemed slightly off-kilter—as if we were poised halfway between this world and that of Mina, Dracula, and the rest. The empty school lot, unfamiliar under the night lights, and the deserted streets added to the feeling.

I was shivering when we got into the car.

Philip threw his coat into the back, and we raced out of the parking lot and flashed over the bridge toward home. The Shostakovich symphony started up again where it had left off, and for a time I lost myself in its rising tension. Philip drove very fast, smiling out into the darkness. Looking at him, I thought how odd it was that we'd really had no real, *personal* conversation. Why? What made Philip different from any other guy?

I was trying to think of a good opening when he slowed for a red light, then spoke. "A good night for vampires, isn't it?"

So he felt that halfway-there feeling too? I grinned at him. "Not much traffic to slow 'em down," I said. "That is, if they have decent wheels. And they must. I mean, I just can't see Dracula driving a beat-up old Volkswagen bus."

"One of the benefits of living eternally is the chance to build your fortune," Philip said, mock-seriously.

"A Rolls for the Count, then," I said. "Definitely conveys the proper image."

"And a private jet. Faster than bat wings."

"For that night skiing in Aspen," I said.

"Blue-blooded dining pleasure afterward," Philip added.

"Then home to the new condo up here in Rocky Bank Estates. I wonder what the neighbors will say?"

"Vampires would make quiet neighbors," Philip assured me as he turned down my street.

"Except for the odd scream or two."

"No, that's the victims of werewolves," he said. "Vampires hypnotize their prey."

"That's right—they go out smiling," I joked. "Well, I can think of worse ways to die, if you have to die. An elegant evening with the vampire of your choice, then instant anemia—"

"The idea is not to be the victim," Philip said slowly, leaning over to adjust the volume on the CD. The Shostakovich symphony had reached its climax, a crash of chords sounding like the thunder of guns. His voice was almost lost in the angry music.

"You mean, *be* a vampire?" I said. "Yuck!"

"Young forever, with the power to make those you love young forever, too?"

"Well, put that way—nice job, if you can get it," I said with a laugh.

"If you can't find them, you send them a signal," he answered, stopping the car in front of my place and turning in his seat to face me. The streetlight slanting across his face shadowed his eyes but highlighted his cheekbones. "A signal strong enough to let them know you're worthy. Then they'll find you." His voice was so smooth, so comforting. I kept playing devil's advocate, to make our conversation last.

"And then you bare your neck and say, 'Soup's on'? No, thanks—besides, I could never give up chocolate."

Philip laughed soundlessly as the music reverberated around us.

"Well, good night, Count," I said, opening the car door.

"Good night, Mina."

Chapter 12

"The show must go on," Mary announced.

Several of us had gathered at morning break near the English department bulletin board. I was relieved to see that what Philip had told me was true: instead of the dreaded cancellation notice, I saw a typed announcement stating that the dress rehearsal would be held tonight.

Mary's eyes went round with dread. "Except whoever hurt Toni is still free. Like *here*—at school."

"I don't think you were ever in any danger." Who'd said that to me? Philip, I remembered. I hadn't thought anything about it at the time, but wasn't it slightly odd? I mean, how did he know? Or was he just trying to make me feel better?

I decided to ask him about it next time I saw him. Then Mary said, "So anyway, guess what ex-gang member they're focusing their attention on?" She heard a step behind us, looked quickly, then flushed red. "Uh-oh," she said under her breath.

I turned to see Frank Donnenfeld saunter up.

"Morning, ladies," he said, smiling sardonically right at Mary.

Mary gave him a slightly pained smile, then said, "Well, speaking of phys ed, time for me to get over there and warm up. Uh, see you later!"

"Later," I said, embarrassed. Frank must have heard what Mary had said.

Frank studied the announcement, his hands in his hip pockets. His back was to me. I hesitated, looking at his ponytail, wondering if I should say something apologetic or not.

"Racked up another fun night down at the station," he said. "I'm thinking of renting a cell there so I can keep a toothbrush and a change of clothes handy."

He'd heard.

"Look, Mary doesn't mean to sound like the jury and judge. She just loves gossip—"

"Of course she does," Frank said, turning to look down at me. "Who doesn't?"

I felt my face go red.

His expression changed. "Hey, I'm sorry," he said suddenly, his tone a lot less full of grade-A attitude. "It was pretty decent of you to try a make-nice. I'm not used to it, and rudeness is kind of a habit."

Thoroughly uncomfortable now, I said, "Uh, well, I'm sorry you got mixed up with the police again."

He shrugged. "See Donnenfeld, dial 911. Unfortunately, I earned that rep, so I guess I have no right to complain." His smile was bright and tight and not really humorous. "So . . . are you going to ask it, or not?"

"Uh, what?" I said—but I knew what he expected.

"No, I didn't throttle that twit, though I did wish for a handy roll of duct tape every time she'd munch down on a fresh wad of gum."

"Well, I wasn't going to ask you that because I remember quite distinctly seeing you standing there in the wings just before she yelled. You have any idea who did do it?"

"Yep."

"Did you tell the police about it?"

"Nope."

"Why not?"

"Because they don't believe a damn word I say, that's why," he said, sounding irritated. "Only reason I'm not cooling my butt in the slammer right now is that they haven't an atom of evidence against me. That and the fact that Toni started accusing Mr. Kane as soon as she woke up. They're having a great time with her, my parole officer told me. She also dragged you into it, but Pilson and half a dozen kids had already said you were onstage when it happened, which is why you didn't join me for the fun and games."

"I'm glad she didn't die, but she really is a first-class fungus."

Frank laughed. "If our boy has a second crack at her when she gets out, I sure as hell won't shed any tears."

" 'Our boy?' "

"I don't know any girls offhand who are strong enough to get the drop on Toni, do you? She's a big girl, and if the rest of her is even half as strong as her jaw muscles, she must have put up a hell of a fight."

I remembered the blackening bruises around her neck and shivered. "So you think it's going to happen again?"

Frank snorted. "You bet it will, and next time he won't screw up."

I rubbed my arms, feeling chilled. The idea that someone was prowling around in the dark, waiting to attack one of us made me want to run home and hide. *"Why?"* I burst out. "It doesn't make any sense!"

Frank looked at his watch and gestured back toward the other buildings. "Bell's going to ring in a minute. I don't know about you, but when I'm late for class, they run a check to see what's missing."

I didn't know whether to laugh or not. He gave me a speculative look, and I noticed his eyes were kind of a greeny-brown behind the glasses. But as we began walking, he went back to the subject. "I'm no shrink, but I learned a lot about the crazies I was locked up with. I recognize the signs of a wacko who's getting desperate. It's going to happen again, and soon, and it's going to be bad."

"I don't think you were ever in any danger." Was I really safe, or was that just Philip thinking the world would be as nice as he was?

"As for why, who knows why lunatics do what they do? It's somehow tied together with this play, that much I've figured out."

The bell rang then, startling us both.

"Have you told anyone any of this?" I asked quickly.

His old derision was back, full force. "You're the only person who's ever listened to me." His expression changed, and he added, "So listen to me now, Jan. Don't go off alone with *anyone*. Anyone at all. Got it?"

He didn't stay to hear my answer; he walked off fast and disappeared around the corner of a building.

I hurried off to my next class, wishing I could leave my thoughts behind me.

Dress rehearsal.

Usually that's enough to cause megadoses of nervousness.

As I got into my tattered crazy-patient costume, I thought about what Frank had said. I'd decided that what Philip had meant was: nobody would attack me because I cooperated, I was reasonable, I didn't cause anyone any grief, as Toni did. My mom had always taught me that when you behave reasonably toward people, eventually they'll do the same by you.

This was how I'd reasoned it all out, but still, as I pulled my costume over my head I did it fast. I didn't like the idea of anyone coming up behind me, not even in the brilliantly lit dressing room full of chattering girls.

Mary and I walked down the hall toward the orchestra pit, where we were supposed to wait. Mary was walking carefully in her filmy vampire lady dress. I noticed that everyone was going around in twos and threes and taking good looks at corners and shadows before passing by them.

"Where's Alyssa?" Heather said to Barbara as Mary and I joined the rest of the cast.

"She'll be here. She had to pick up her dress from the cleaner's."

"Why aren't we onstage?" William asked, staring at the empty set waiting for actors.

"Pilson wants to talk to us first," Glen said.

"Oh, great. What now?"

"Shhh—here he comes."

Mr. Pilson bustled in, looking more nervous than ever.

"Students, the principal and the police are now satisfied that the accidents were caused by a criminal who must have come in from outside. We are keeping the outer doors locked at all times now, so if you need to go out for any reason, tell us, and we can let you back in. They also asked me to extend apologies to anyone who might have been made uncomfortable during the necessary questioning."

This incredible understatement netted no more than a snort from some of the kids, and a sarcastic look from Frank. Mary looked around with a slightly nervous hunch to her shoulders, and Heather and Susan exchanged looks. Near them, Philip leaned against a chair, looking like some kind of royal painting in that handsome black and white tuxedo. His expression was distracted.

"Now, as soon as our leading lady gets here, I'll go lock the door—"

Boom!

That was the outer door.

Heads whipped around as Alyssa rushed in, almost running down the aisle. She carried four dresses in floating plastic over one arm. "Sorry I'm late," she said brightly. "I had to pick these up from the cleaner's."

As soon as she reached her usual spot in the front row, she threw the dresses over the back of an empty chair and picked up her copy of the play. "I'll just go and get dressed, and look at my lines while I—"

She stopped, her face going white. Then she screamed and flung the book on the floor as if it were a spider.

"What's this?" Mr. Pilson twittered, picking up her play. "Goodness." Heather and Susan went and stood next to Alyssa and asked her what was wrong.

Glen got up and leaned over the teacher's shoulder, and several kids followed suit. "Oooh, a death threat!"

"What's it say? What's it say?" Heather demanded.

" 'If you go onstage opening night, you will not live past moonrise the next night,' " Glen read, and whistled.

"Why the brown ink?" William asked. "It looks kind of messy."

"It's not brown ink, that's blood!" Glen said.

Mary gave a little shriek. "I don't want to see it." She covered her eyes.

"Students! Sit down!" Mr. Pilson called. Turning to Alyssa, he asked, "Where did this come from?"

"I didn't put it there!" she snapped. As utter silence fell, she turned and pointed her finger right in my face. "There's the one who did it—the one who's been trying to get me thrown out of the play."

Chapter 13

"*What?*" I gasped.

"Want a witness for your slander lawsuit, Jan?" Frank cut in, face hard and arms folded.

"You probably wrote it yourself!" Mary flashed at Alyssa.

Students started yelling insults back and forth, until Mr. Pilson, his face crimsom with anger, shouted, "QUIET! You settle down right now, and if we have any more trouble, I'll ask the principal to cancel the play." He turned to me. "Do you know anything about this?"

"No," I said, my voice shaking with anger. I looked directly into Alyssa's face. "I'm not in the habit of putting blood all over people's things."

Alyssa flushed.

Mr. Pilson said, "Did anyone see this paper being put into Alyssa's notebook?"

No one spoke. Mr. Pilson sighed. "Perhaps it was someone outside of the Drama Club. It's an unfortunate prank, but we have to put it aside right now."

Philip looked up and spoke: "Why don't we get started?"

With a venomous glare at me, Alyssa snatched up her costumes and said, "I'll get dressed."

As people began moving about, Barbara came up

next to me. "You really don't know anything about that note?"

Alyssa's accusation had totally stunned me. When Barbara spoke, anger rushed through me again and I turned to say something really annihilating. Then I saw her expression and stopped.

She didn't look accusing—she looked worried.

So I just said, "No. Of course not. What makes you think I did?"

Her brows drew together, then she shook her head quickly. "Oh, just—there are a few things going on that bother me." She gave a quick smile. "Not that I mean to act like some kind of know-it-all. It's just . . ."

"Well?"

"You've been out with Philip a few times, haven't you?"

"We've had two practices. Why?"

Her eyes strayed over to where Philip stood talking with Glen and Paul, and she sighed. "The play's really important to him, isn't it?"

"Well, isn't it important to us all? What are you getting at?"

"Nothing," she said doubtfully, then she shook her head. "Never mind. Just, you know—be careful."

"Act One, Scene One—places!" Mr. Pilson called.

Barbara hurried away to get onstage, her lacy dress ruffling out behind her. I frowned. What had she been getting at?

The rehearsal started off slowly. William got nervous and stumbled on his lines when the lighting people missed their cues and switched the spots back and forth. Mr. Pilson stopped one scene and started it again, which made Alyssa mad. She did it, but she stomped around and said her lines in a hard, angry voice.

When Philip came on, I felt the first stirrings of magic. It wasn't just me, either; the art students in the back who were finishing up the last touches on props stopped what they were doing and drifted to the wings to watch.

He and Glen were really good together, and when Barbara as Lucy began to feel the mental pull, her transformation from a flirty girl into a vampire was so well done, it gave me shivers.

When Alyssa came on, I could tell Philip had tried to show her some of the restaging that he and I had worked out. Some of it she did; other parts she forgot or ignored and went back to Ms. Slater's staging. Alyssa's long, filmy gowns were great, and she knew all her lines—but whenever she was onstage, she just looked like a spoiled teenager in dress-up, and the magic drained from the scene.

I could feel the reaction of the people watching. Mr. Pilson hovered, looking helpless, and the kids in the wings whispered. When Frank came onstage, things got better. With his frock coat and boots and his long hair dusted with gray, Frank really did look like an adventurous professor of the Indiana Jones type. His quest to unmask and kill the vampire seemed single-minded in intensity—and Philip's performance gained power as he baited and mocked and challenged.

The magic stirred again—but in the scene when

Dracula issues his challenge to the men chasing him by luring Mina and trying to make her drink his blood, everything went flat. Mina pouted and shrugged and—suddenly we were high school kids strutting around on a stage again.

After the scene Frank shook his head and disappeared backstage. Philip also disappeared from view, but I saw him again almost immediately when he walked slowly near where I'd placed a chair so I could watch the play.

"You're great," I whispered to him.

He'd been studying the ground. At the sound of my voice, he looked up, frowning and angry. "Not good enough."

"What? No way!"

He shook his head, then looked up at the lights. His face was taut with tension. "It's Alyssa," he said. "She's the problem."

"Well, at least it's not because of you that the magic isn't working."

"Magic?" he asked.

"Yes. The whatever-it-is that makes a play come alive."

He studied me intently. "So you know it, too," he said slowly.

I shrugged. "Any good actor knows it."

"No, they don't," he said. "Not when it comes alive. It's . . . rare. But it happens. I've—read about it. And I've tried, but I haven't been strong enough." These last words were spoken softly and quickly, as if to himself.

"Look," I said. "You're good—really good. Every-

126

one watching us is going to believe in you. Don't worry about Alyssa. I think they'll take it into consideration."

"They," he repeated slowly, his eyes distant. Then he frowned, his whole body taut with tension. "I can't take that chance," he said. Sweat gleamed on his brow, making his fine dark hair stick to his forehead. He lifted a shaking hand to brush his hair back, then abruptly turned away and disappeared down the corridor.

I thought of running after him to warn him not to go alone—but I figured he was strong enough to take care of himself. In the meantime, I shook my head, thinking to myself that some actors took dress rehearsal all too seriously.

We went through Act Three twice all the way through, and everyone except Alyssa got marginally better. She pouted her way through the second run-through, yawning from time to time. Once, when Mr. Pilson stopped the action and asked her not to giggle after a certain line, she muttered—just loud enough for everyone to hear—"Ms. Slater never treated me like that." I felt sorry for her right then: I knew that she would never have what it takes to be an actress. No matter who her dad was or how good-looking she was.

Except for Alyssa, the mood was fairly good when at last we ended. It was going to be a strong play. Not a great one, unfortunately, but a good one. The students gathering around Frank and Glen and Philip and Barbara made it clear who they thought were talented.

The actors seemed exhilarated, in a way I knew and missed. I could hardly get that same feeling from my walk-on, so I struggled with my familiar jealousy battle. I heard some of the others deciding to go celebrate at the diner hangout, but I told myself it was already late enough for a bus ride across town.

Muttering a "See you tomorrow" to Mary, I went to the dressing room and changed, then left. As I walked toward the bus stop, a flicker of white caught my eye, and I saw the flutter of Alyssa's gorgeous white gown that she wore in the last act. The wind tore at it as she got into a familiar black car—Philip's Jaguar. A moment later I saw him, still in his Count Dracula tuxedo, walk quickly around to the driver's door and get in.

So he was going to give her some last-ditch coaching. He was going back to her. She had won.

A moment later, I heard footsteps on the sidewalk behind me, and there was Frank. "Going to the diner?" he asked.

I shook my head, retying my scarf as the winds tried to snatch it away. "The bus ride is long enough without waiting until when they only come once an hour."

He half-turned away, hesitated, then said carelessly, "My bike is faster than a bus." By now, I was no longer fooled by the supposed indifference. He really did care what people said to him and about him—cared enough to build up a wall to protect himself.

"And a jet is faster than a bike," I said, realizing

suddenly that I didn't care about his past. I liked the Frank I'd gotten to know a little during the play. "Is that a general observation or an offer?"

"Whichever."

I laughed. "Got a spare helmet?"

"You'll wear mine."

He fitted a shiny black helmet over my head, and though it was too big, at least it kept the icy wind off my ears when he gunned the bike and we rolled down the road and over the bridge.

He was careful not to speed, but still the winds tore through my clothes and made my hands numb. After a mile or two, he had to stop at a red light.

He turned around to look at me. Jerking his thumb at a neon-lit coffee shop across the street, he said, "Want a quick cup of hot chocolate or something?"

"Sure," I said through chattering teeth.

He turned the motorcycle and pulled into the parking lot. As soon as we got inside, he said, "Are you okay? Maybe this was a stupid idea."

"It's fun," I said. "Don't mind my teeth—something warm will fix me up. I've never been on one of those things before."

He led the way to a booth, and as soon as we'd ordered, he said, "What did you think?"

"The play?" At his nod, I said, "Good, for the most part. Too bad about Alyssa."

"Did anyone strike you as out of it? Anyone besides Alyssa, I mean."

"Out of it?"

He lifted a shoulder in an impatient shrug. "Weird vibes."

129

"Performance? Or—"

"Anything."

I thought of the scene backstage. "Philip was upset about how lousy Alyssa is. He seemed to think it was his fault."

"How well do you know that guy?" Frank asked abruptly.

The waitress appeared then, which kept me from answering. I put my cold hands around my cup of hot chocolate, then leaned down to slurp the whipped cream off the top before it melted. Halfway through this, I realized that these were the manners I used with my family, but they weren't exactly cool when I was actually out with a guy. I looked up.

Frank grinned at me over the steaming coffee cup that he held cradled in his hands. "Go ahead. Don't mind me."

So I slurped the rest of the whipped cream, then tried a scalding mouthful of the chocolate. Looking up through tear-stung eyes, I saw Frank waiting—and I remembered his question.

"I don't really *know* him," I said. "I've spent some time with him, and we did talk about other stuff besides the play, if that's what you're wondering. Though not much, I admit." I smiled, thinking that if I had gone out with Philip, I wouldn't have been tempted to slurp whipped cream.

Frank's eyes narrowed consideringly, and he said, "Were you always on your best behavior with him?"

"I thought you wouldn't mind if I slurped," I joked, but his face stayed serious. "What do you mean, 'best behavior'? Philip himself is the formal type. Is that a crime?"

"No, *that* isn't a crime," Frank said slowly, looking at me.

I drew back in surprise. "Look, you can't be hinting that Philip is the one who strangled Toni. If you are, I just don't believe it. So I think we'd better drop the conversation."

"All right, then. We'll drop it."

"You *do* think it," I said. *"Why?"*

"You don't want to drop it?"

"Just tell me why you think he did that to Toni."

"Strangled Toni and nailed Kane with the wire— *and* fixed Slater's brakes, and carved her up a little while he was at it."

"You're crazy," I said, staring at him, feeling sick inside. "No *way*. I've spent time with him—he just couldn't. No way. He's one of the gentlest people I know."

"Did he tell you all about his past? Ask you anything about yours?" Frank asked.

I shook my head slowly, more in denial of his words than in answer to his questions. "It wasn't, like, a date —we were working on the play."

"Well, *why* is what I can't figure," he said. "If it *is* him, it's all tied in with this play, but I don't know how."

"It just doesn't fit! He's sensitive and kind. . . ."

"Who else, then?"

"Who says that all those things were done by the same person? Have the police said so?"

"Pretty much. They spent about six hours accusing me of all of it the other night."

"It just doesn't make sense," I said. "Of all the people in the play, he's the one who's never said anything bad about anyone. Heck, I'd believe Mary did it —or Alyssa, for that matter—before I'd believe it was Philip."

Frank frowned into his coffee. "What did he say when you talked backstage?"

I repeated the conversation as much as I could remember, right up to seeing Philip and Alyssa leave together. Frank listened without interrupting, then shrugged and leaned back into his seat.

"You're right. Doesn't sound especially threatening to me, either. Maybe the part about Alyssa being the problem . . ."

"No," I said. "You're wrong."

"Well, maybe so. I've been wrong before," he said. A ghost of his usual irony curved his lips. "One thing I gotta say, I thought high school drama would be boring, but so far it's been anything but."

"What made you—uh, how did you get into it?"

He grinned. "You don't have to pussyfoot around about my record. I spent seven years breaking into people's homes and stealing cars. I got caught once too often and did a stretch at the state youth facility. I don't do it anymore."

"Just like that?"

"Just like that," he said. "I took a good look at my uncle, the one who trained me, and realized he wasn't a cool guy in cool clothes. He was a mean, small-time hood, and soon he was going to be a middle-aged small-time hood. I don't want to be like him. So I won't."

"So you picked the stage?"

Frank grinned. "I directed a play, mostly by accident, at the Pit—ah, that's what we called the state youth facility. Discovered I really liked it, although when I get out of Cresswell, I think I'd like to mess around with some film classes. I don't know. First I gotta get out of here." He drank off his coffee and set the cup down. "How about you?"

"Stage," I said. "I love the theater. And, well, I kind of like the idea of trying to write my own plays."

"You're good," he said, jabbing a finger at me. "Don't let the bozos like Alyssa get to you. They'll use every weapon they have to cover a total lack of talent."

"That's what my mother says."

"Smart mom."

"Speaking of whom . . ."

"Right. We're outta here."

He got up and threw a crumpled dollar onto the table. He paid at the register, and soon we were on our way through the town. This time I didn't freeze so badly, and when we pulled up in front of my place, my hands were just chilled.

"Thanks," I called softly, handing his helmet back. He smiled, jammed the helmet on his head, and rode away.

When I got inside, my mother stood there in her nightgown, looking tired and a little disapproving. "It's late," she said.

"Dress rehearsal. Went out for hot chocolate after."

"Oh," she said, rubbing her eyes. "Well, I was about to tell him you were gone when I heard you come in."

"Him?" I said, feeling a peculiar lurch inside.

"Phone," Mome said, pointing. "He's still on."

I walked to the table and picked up the receiver. "Hello?" I said cautiously.

"Hi," said Philip's soft voice. "Would you like to go out for a drive?"

"When?"

"Right now."

Chapter 14

"Uh, it's late," I said, looking back over my shoulder. My mother was just disappearing up the stairs. "I'm sorry, I don't think I can."

"I must talk to you. It's important."

"Can't we talk like this, over the phone?" I asked.

At the top of the stairs I heard my mother say, "Jan? It's bedtime."

"Coming, Mom," I called. "Look, Philip, I gotta go. Can it wait?"

"Yes," he said. "It can wait."

Relieved, I said good-bye and hung up. My heart was banging away in my ribs as if I'd done a marathon in football gear. I hadn't believed anything Frank had said about Philip earlier—so why was I scared?

Because it's late, I thought, going upstairs. I went into my room and realized there was no way I'd be able to sleep, so I decided to take a hot bath. I was just starting to get out of my clothes when I heard the phone ring.

One leg was out of my jeans. I jammed my foot back in and hopped to the landing. My mother's door stayed closed. She was already asleep.

I was on the first step when I heard the answering machine click on. *"Hi, this is Barbara. I got your number from Mary. I'm calling around to find out if Alyssa's with anyone."*

I reached the bottom of the stairs and zoomed toward the kitchen.

"She's not home yet, and so we're checking around," Barbara's voice went on. "I still gotta call Frank and Paul—so g'bye!"

I skidded into the kitchen and got my hand on the receiver just as I heard her hang up. A loud dial tone buzzed, then the machine clicked off. I thought of trying to get her number from Information; then I remembered that she had others to call.

I wasn't willing to sit there and wait who knew how long until her phone wasn't busy, just to say I didn't know where Alyssa was. I hadn't seen her since she got into Philip's car after the rehearsal. So I decided to go upstairs and take that bath.

I was out in the hall again when I heard a noise in the living room. I paused to look and saw a movement in the darkness that shifted, then resolved into a tall male silhouette. I froze, my mouth open to scream, when the figure came toward me. A slanted beam of light fell on a snow-white shirt and a vest with diamond studs glittering on it, above which was Philip's face.

"Hey," I gasped. "How the heck did you get in here?"

"I can get in anywhere," he said in his deep, smooth voice. Scarlet flashed; the lining of his long cloak as he flung one side back over his shoulder.

"What are—"

"I can't wait anymore," he said. "It has to be now. You've got to help me with Lucy."

"Lucy?"

He blinked, then shook his head a little. "The last rehearsal," he said, stepping closer, taking my hands. "The last one before the real performance. You've got to be there. You're the only other person who can make it real."

The light from the kitchen slanted across his eyes, which despite the marks of exhaustion were steady and patient and gentle.

"I need you," he said, "like the Count needs Mina."

"It's just that it's so *late*. Oh! I saw you with Alyssa, and they're calling around, trying to find her. Do you know where she is?"

"Yes. She's somewhere safe."

"Somewhere? Safe?" I repeated.

"Yes. Will you help me with her?"

"Help with her—like how?"

"Free her."

I gasped. "Is she stuck somewhere? Is she okay? Have you called the police?"

"We have to go before it's too late."

"Wait a minute! Who—*what*—"

"I'll explain on the way." He was still holding my hands in his strong grip. With a slow, deliberate movement he raised one hand and bowed his head over it. A lock of his hair drifted into his eyes as his lips brushed, gentle and warm, over my hand.

Blood pounded in my ears. Someone else's voice seemed to be speaking: "I—we—my jacket—"

A jewel on his shirt cuff gave a muted cobalt flash as he raised his hand and undid the clasp. With a quick movement he swung his cape around my shoulders. Its unfamiliar weight swathed me with warmth.

"Come, we must go now."

His fingers closed around mine. With his other hand he opened the French doors to the little terrace.

"I think I should at least leave a note or something," I said weakly, shoving my feet into a pair of old shoes I kept by the kitchen door. I hardly noticed what I was doing. "I should tell my mom."

"Why disturb anyone?" His arm slid around my shoulders, and through the velvet of the cape and his jacket and shirt, his muscles were as hard as steel. His eyes burned directly into mine, and I forgot everything else as I fell under his spell again. "You are safe with me," he said.

And I *felt* safe. We'd switched into the play world again, the strange world of Mina and the Count. I didn't even feel the chill as I pulled the cape around me and got into the car.

This time the music was singing, and I recognized the ominous and unearthly Mozart *Requiem*. The voices swelled and softened, shifting keys moodily as they sang the ancient Latin words. The bewitchment was powerful; I didn't realize how fast Philip was driving until he sped right through a red light.

I grabbed the dashboard—but nothing was coming from the opposite direction. Philip gave me a quick smile. "You're safe," he said again.

"Not when you drive so fast," I said nervously.

"We'll soon be able to drive as fast as we like."

I almost didn't hear his voice as the music rose to a

crescendo. Then the car swept around a corner, and we raced over the Swenson Bridge toward school.

School? I didn't know what I'd expected, but school wasn't it. Surprise, mixed with relief at the sight of familiar buildings, kept me silent as we pulled into the parking lot. Of course! Philip and Alyssa had gone out to eat, then came back to practice, using Philip's key to get in. Nothing sinister there.

It was the last comforting thought I was to have for a very long time.

"Did Alyssa somehow manage to lock herself into the bathroom or something?" I asked.

Philip keyed open the front door, we went in, and he locked the deadbolt behind us.

"*They* don't heed locks," he said softly. "When They've been invited in. And soon, you and I will not heed locks either."

That was the first time I really registered the captial T in *They*. Getting a distinctly bad feeling about it, I said, "They? As in audience?"

"Will you still have Them watch us?" he asked. "I wouldn't mind it."

Hoo boy, I said under my breath. *Either I'm cracking up, or—Or HE is . . .* and I remembered what Frank had said—and Barbara had tried to say. But one look at Philip's compelling smile, and I got confused again.

Meanwhile, Philip had taken my hand, and he led me swiftly through the pitch-dark auditorium. He certainly knew his way.

"Look, can't we just find Alyssa and talk about this tomorrow?" I said calmly. *Be reasonable, and people will be reasonable back.* "There's nothing that can't be fixed tomorrow, and I'm sure Alyssa would listen if we, like, held a vote of the other actors or something. I mean, for the sake of the play, and"—I blushed—"you, I'll do Mina."

"Listen," he cautioned. "They come."

I shut up; Philip wasn't hearing me anyway. He stopped, and except for our breathing, I heard nothing.

" 'Tis now the very witching time of night,' " he said softly. " 'When churchyards yawn and hell itself breathes out contagion in this world. I could drink hot blood—' "

I recognized the lines from *Hamlet*, and let me tell you, they did nothing to quiet my growing confusion. What was Philip doing? Was he crazy? Was I crazy? *Frank, where are you?*

Some of Ophelia's lines came to me, the words she spoke when she first realized Hamlet was going crazy, and I tried to catch his attention:

" 'Now see that noble and most sovereign reason . . .' "

Philip laughed. "Don't cry woe, for unlike Hamlet and Ophelia we'll soon have immortal youth."

He found the backstage steps somehow, and we went racing up, me stumbling once. He pulled me to my feet without any effort at all, which didn't encourage me to think my new plan of yanking my hand free and just running for it would work.

Besides, I could hear noises now: a thumping sound, and a muffled voice crying unevenly.

Philip stopped, reached for something, and a yellow light flared on, making the shadows jump back.

Philip's eyes were wide and direct, his pupils black, their intensity scaring me a little. "She won't listen to me," he said. "You must talk to her. Tell her to be calm, and there will be no pain. She'll be free of this world, and her flight will signal Them that we are here, and ready."

"What? Who?" I babbled.

Philip pulled me up more stairs, to a narrow hallway just above the backstage area. On one side was a small row of little rooms, and on the other a rail divided us from the stage far below. Huge lights loomed around us.

This must be where the lighting people went to change the lights, and the rooms would be where they kept their equipment, I thought numbly. The noises were louder now, coming from the middle room.

The light from below outlined Philip's jaw and the upper part of his eye ridge, leaving his eyes in shadow. His taut face was skull-like for a moment as he paused, listening. Then he said, "She won't be reasonable. You must convince her. I will wait here for you."

"Wait?" I heard Alyssa scream behind the door. "Who's there? Let me OUT! Philip, I'm sorry, I'm sorry, I'll leave your stupid play, I promise, I never liked it anyway, I just want yo-ooooou . . ." Her voice ended on loud, rising sobs. "Please! This isn't funny!"

Philip let go of me, one hand reaching for the lock.

A wild idea of grabbing the keys from his hand flitted through my brain, then died, like moths in a fire, when I saw his other hand touch his sleeve, reach in—and pull out a long, gleaming knife.

141

Chapter 15

I stared in shock at the knife. It finally, finally, filtered into my brain who was the danger—who it had been all along. And I was alone with him.

"Go to her, Mina," he said softly. "Bring her out. We will perform the blood ritual together, and share immortality."

I swallowed with a very dry throat, my heart trying to thump its way out of my ribs as he unlatched the door.

I had about two seconds to think of a plan.

Alyssa gasped as I felt my way into the little storage room. "Alyssa," I whispered desperately, not daring to turn around to see if he was listening or not. "He's gone batso, and he's got a knife, but the two of us together can probably—"

The door let in a slanting ray of pale light. A figure moved, and the light fell across Alyssa's face. It was smeared with tears and makeup and dust. Her blotchy eyes widened as they lit on me, then narrowed in fury.

"YOU!" she spat out. "You put him up to this! I'll *kill* you!"

She lunged at me, her fingers hooked like claws.

"Alyssa, listen! He's got a—"

I tried to block her, but she had the momentum. She shoved me hard against the wall. My head crashed backward against a metal shelf, making lights flash across my vision. I grabbed at her, but my hands felt empty air.

I fell on my knees. The world spun sickeningly as I watched Alyssa run past.

She launched herself at the tall figure in immaculate black. For a moment they were framed in the doorway, the white-gowned figure struggling madly against the other holding the knife. The scuffle lasted only a moment, the outcome inevitable; the tall figure was so much stronger than the girl in white. I saw a cold flash of metal. Alyssa shrieked with a high, bubbly sound and lunged again—then Philip lifted his hands and stepped back.

I saw Alyssa hit the rail, scrabble at it with her hands, then go over. A long sickening moment, then the hard thud as she hit the stage. Followed by silence.

I got up slowly, fighting dizziness and pain. Something sticky and warm trickled down the back of my scalp. I shuddered, afraid to feel the cut I knew was there, and stood up. The long hem of Philip's cloak almost tripped me; I stumbled, then made it to the door.

A shadow moved in front of me. Squinting through the still-spinning world, I saw Philip watching me, his breathing coming in short pants, his hair hanging in his eyes. His hand lifted toward me, and I saw a red smear along the edge of the knife.

"You should have said to her what I told you to say."

"Philip, what you said makes no *sense*," I said carefully. Slowly. "None of this is fun. As far as I'm concerned, the game is over, and so's the play. There's been an accident. We need to call for help—"

"We won't need the play to bring them," he said. "They'll come now. Her blood will call them—"

"Philip," I said desperately, *"this* is real. Not that play. There are no vampires."

Wrong answer, Matthis.

His eyes narrowed. "Are you then my enemy?"

"No!" I yelled.

" 'You, Madame Mina, crime touches you not. Your mind works true,' " he quoted, reaching for me.

I backed away. "Listen to me, Philip. Let's drop the Mina and Count game. What's real on stage *ends* when you step off the stage—you know that. You *must* know that!"

Philip advanced, step by step, and I backed into the darkness of the hallway, finding it friendly compared with the danger before me. Philip paused to strike his hair out of his eyes, and I turned and ran.

Four, five steps I took before he caught up with me. I fought to get free, but he got a steely arm around me and held me against him. "If you will not change with me, then I must give you the world of silence," he said, close to my ear.

I heard a click as he laid the knife down on the rail, and then his hands closed around my neck.

I kicked and fought, and I tried to draw in enough breath to scream, but nothing worked. My lungs burned for air and the world started fading—

And miraculously, the hands loosened in a sudden movement.

I realized I'd heard a voice. Not Philip's, another voice—strong, mocking, from somewhere below.

"Well, nightwalker? Afraid of my challenge?" It was Frank Donnenfeld.

Philip laughed soundlessly, looking up, his eyes very wide and silver. "Van Helsing," he said. "No wonder They have not come."

He took my hand, and with his other hand he grabbed up his knife. Pulling me to the narrow stairway and down, he struck off the lights with the knifehilt, plunging us in darkness once more.

I tried to free my hand, couldn't, and so I stumbled after Philip, gasping, feeling sick and dizzy, trying to slow him down. We ran down hallways I couldn't see and didn't know, then down another stairway to an area that smelled dusty and unused. The air was shockingly cold, and my body felt numb.

"He will not find us here—" came a whisper against my ear.

Not three seconds later Frank's voice echoed, "Afraid of the sun? I can wait. Can you?"

Philip's body tensed, and once more we had to run, at a headlong pace down more steps and across a room filled with unknown bulky objects. I cried out when a large box jutted against my hip bone as we ran, but Philip didn't slow down. A light went on across a room; the objects became discarded sets. Dust swirled around my feet, and beside me Philip looked wild-eyed and excited.

In the distance I heard the eerie wail of sirens. Police.

"'And so, you would play your brains against

" " Philip said in the Count's voice, his teeth
⸻e in a terrible grin. " 'You will know now what it
is to cross my will.' "

Philip yanked my hand violently, and we began to
run again. He found a door that closed us once more
into blackness. Tears began to burn down my face.
"Philip, please—" I heard footsteps following, and
then a call:

"I know this place, nightwalker. And I've got a
stake."

Philip stopped, then changed direction abruptly.
Overhead came the sounds of many running feet.
Shouts came, indistinct: "Where are they?"

"Down here!"

Philip closed his hands on a steel door, and again
we ran. My breath was coming in short gasps, I was
almost sobbing, and my throat ached worse than my
head. I wondered what he would do if I just passed
out, right on his heels. I considered it. It would be
such a relief.

Suddenly he stopped, pulling me close against him.
The edge of the knife touched my neck. "Be silent,"
he breathed into my ear.

"No lights down here," a voice called.

"Where's another flash?"

Footsteps and voices drew near—then passed by,
fading into a rumble. Philip gave a quiet laugh of tri-
umph, his breath stirring my hair. " 'They played
their wits against me—I who have commanded na-
tions.' "

It was Dracula's line again. Philip was thoroughly
Dracula now. Despite my headache and the blood

running down the back of my neck, I knew I had to think of a plan. Some kind of plan, anything to get him to be Philip again. *Maybe Philip Devereux is one taco short on his combination plate*, I thought, trying to rally myself, *but he is a heck of a sight better than when he's Dracula.*

We went up some stairs, and then I groaned, choking on my sobs; "I have to rest—I can't run any . . . farther."

"It's quiet here," he said. "We'll fly anon."

"You said . . . you'd left signs," I gasped.

"Signs?"

"You know. Signals. To warn the—uh, vampires."

"Signs," he drew the word out, sounding confused. Then he said, "Kane and Slater. But they didn't work. That's why we were going to use Lucy tonight."

"Kane? Slater?" I repeated the teachers' names, hoping to get his mind back to the here-and-now.

"Come. I hear Van Helsing's pursuit again." He tugged on me, and I got wearily to my feet. "My bearings . . . my bearings . . ." He muttered to himself, then plunged off in one direction. "Where are They hiding?"

The run in the darkness was a nightmare, and so were my aching head and neck, but nothing was worse than the calm, pleasant voice describing how he had planned every step of Ms. Slater's death. Right down to watching her crash and cutting her throat and drinking her blood. I clapped a hand across my mouth, trying not to throw up.

The noises outside got close again. "Hey, look! Footprints in the dust here."

"All right, let's take a look. You two over there . . ."

Abruptly Philip stopped, pressed us into some dusty, rotting material, and held his knife against my neck.

The footsteps clomped nearer and nearer—I pulled my breath in silently, hoping for a chance to scream, and the knife tightened at my neck. Tears began running down my cheeks again, hot and stinging, as the footsteps passed us by. Silence.

Philip shifted his grip on me and bent close. "Now we'll—"

"Now we'll step into the sunlight, bucko."

Frank. My heart sang. A moment later a light turned on, bright and strong. I winced, blinded, and Philip's hand jerked on my arm. He pulled me hard against him, and once more I felt the cold edge of his knife at my neck.

"Now we'll die together," he said, looking up at Frank, who came slowly down some rickety wooden stairs.

My vision came back, weirdly hazy. We were in another storage area, this one full of old furniture. Frank moved slowly, his hands out from his sides, his jeans and denim jacket splashed with mud.

Frank kept his eyes on Philip, who was absolutely still behind me.

"Make you a deal," Frank said suddenly.

Philip said nothing. He hardly breathed.

"Let her go. You want blood? Come get mine," Frank invited.

"No—" I started.

The knife tightened, and Frank's glasses flashed as his eyes switched from me back to Philip.

"Come on." Frank grinned a mocking challenge. "I'm not armed, and I've got lots more of the red stuff than she does." He stepped down the last step and sauntered toward us.

Philip moved fast. He flung me away and lunged at Frank.

"Right answer, rich boy," Frank snarled, and attacked.

Philip was certainly strong, and he probably knew how to fight, but he hadn't been on the streets for seven years, learning every dirty trick there was in order to survive. The fight lasted only seconds, then Frank sent Philip sprawling backward. His head cracked hard on the edge of a table and he slumped, motionless, the knife spinning away from his loosened grip.

Somebody was crying, sobbing like a little kid. About the time I realized it was me, Frank had his arms around me. "Hey, hey. You're okay. It's over."

A moment later a door behind us burst open and a voice shouted: "Freeze!"

Police swarmed in, yelling questions and commands, but neither of us noticed. I tried to choke down my pent-up tears, and Frank went on hugging me until he discovered Philip's cloak still around my shoulders after all this time, and with a violent movement he ripped it free and flung it away.

Chapter 16

"So how have you been?"

Frank dropped onto the seat opposite me in the coffee shop booth.

"Tired, mostly," I said.

"You haven't been at school."

"The doctor said I had a mild concussion from where Alyssa slammed me. I'm supposed to stay home and rest. Ha. Fat chance."

He smiled briefly, then said, "I tried calling."

"I know. Mom told me, but she wasn't letting me talk to anyone that I didn't *have* to."

"Wondered if it was just me. You know, 'Thanks—now get lost.'"

I sighed. "Mom never prejudges. You'll see when you get to know her. She really was trying to guard me from extra hassles. It was bad enough with all those questions the police asked, and then that psychiatrist the district attorney appointed for Philip, and then one sent by the school for *my* sake."

"Was it pretty bad?"

"Medium bad," I said, rubbing my eyes. "I think the worst, though, was when Philip's uncle came himself, just to apologize. He was sweet and courtly and all, but you know, he seems as out of the world as Philip—almost."

"Met him at Alyssa's funeral."

I shuddered. "Was he wiped out?"

"Poor old geezer. He was real upset, kept trying to apologize to everyone and anyone, but the Perrys wouldn't even talk to him."

"Building up for their lawsuit," I said.

Frank shook his head, looking disgusted. "Well, they can try for the big bucks, but I don't know that they'll win. My parole officer told me yesterday that Alyssa died from a broken neck. The cut Philip gave her wasn't lethal."

"Alyssa's dad came to visit me in the hospital," I said. "I was still pretty out of it, but I think he was trying to tell me that my accident was all my fault—in case I was thinking of lawsuits against *them.*"

Frank laughed. It wasn't a nice laugh. "He also came by the station when I was there and as much as blamed me for not having saved his daughter. The mother was worse. No wonder Alyssa was such a mess, with parents like that."

"I still feel sorry for her," I said. "I wish I'd been able to do something. But you know, I've been thinking about it. In her own way she was as crazy as Philip, the way she expected everyone to instantly fall in with her plans. She just wasn't violent about it. I wasn't a real person to her, just something in her way. Anyone else would have listened to me when I came into that storage room. Even Toni—I think. She came to apologize, by the way. It wasn't very gracious, but she tried."

"Maybe all of us had some trouble seeing reality," Frank said.

"If you mean me and Philip, you're right," I said. "I've thought a lot about that, too. I got mad at Glen for judging me on externals—my street and my clunky house—and I did just the opposite with Philip. If he hadn't been so, oh, cool-looking, with that car and the money and manners and all, maybe I would have realized something was wrong. You and Barbara saw it, all right, but I just went along with him because I thought he liked me, not my performance of Mina."

Frank shrugged, looking down at his coffee. " 'The play's the thing.' "

The unexpected quote made me shiver. "I've had enough Shakespeare," I said. "I still can't get over the fact that when he meant the play would be real, he meant *real*. He really thought that vampires would come, and that he'd get to become one. He was crazy. And I fell for his act, just like a total idiot."

"But it wasn't an act," Frank said. "He believed in it. That kind of craziness mixed with all that talent is real convincing. Look at Hitler and Germany in World War II."

"And Charles Manson," I said. "I know, the school psych pointed all that out. I still feel bad, and I guess I'm just going to have to work it all out in my own mind. Anyway, while I was talking to the shrink appointed by the district attorney, I found out some stuff about Philip's past. It's sad, really. He was an only child, and his parents dragged him all over Europe while they did big money deals and social stuff with counts and dukes and powerful business magnates. He grew up in hotels, never had any real friends. He was closest to his mother, but when she died, his uncle said he just, like, withdrew. The father tried coping for a short time, and when someone at his private school suggested he be institutionalized because he was showing signs of schizophrenia, the father wouldn't have any of that. No one in the great Devereux family has mental problems! *Those* are for *poor* people."

"Guy sounds like a head case himself."

"That's what I think. So anyway, the dad sent Philip to the uncle and didn't tell him why. Said it was for a change of scene. The uncle didn't know what was wrong—he'd never had any kids of his own, and Philip seemed such a quiet, well-mannered kid."

"Quiet and well-mannered—and carried around a six-inch hunting knife in a wrist sheath," Frank said, shaking his head.

"And used his own blood to write that threatening letter to Alyssa. I think I'm going to have nightmares about him for a year."

"Whole thing is a drag," Frank said. "He'll never get out of the funny farm now."

"Who knows?" I said, and shuddered again. "If he does, I hope it's in some other country." Vivid images of that seemingly endless night flashed through my mind, ending with the fight in the storage room. Frank's jacket covered with mud. I looked up at him. "What nobody told me was, how you managed to get there so fast?"

Frank shrugged. "I went home after I dropped you off that night, and when I got there my kid brother told me some girl had called, wanting to know where Alyssa was. I remembered what you'd told me about seeing them together, and then"—he shrugged again—"I just had a feeling. Got back on my bike and raced to school. I told you I didn't know right away what was wrong, but I knew it tied in with the play somehow. I figured whatever was going on would be at the auditorium. Got it in one: saw his car right out front. Had my keys on me, since I'd been cleaning just the night before after a PTA bash. Let myself in. Heard voices down front, ran for the stage. Got there just in time to see Alyssa take her dive."

"Did you try . . . ?"

He nodded. "You bet I did. Saw all that blood all over, her head was lying at a bad angle, and I knew enough not to touch her. I ran back to the lobby, dialed 911 on the phone there, got back just in time to hear you choking up there on the skywalk. So I did the first thing that came into my head—yelled one of Van Helsing's lines at him. Trying to get his attention."

"It worked," I said. "He was really into vampire mode then."

"Vampire," Frank repeated, giving a low whistle. "Never guessed that. And that business with him carving up the Slater witch, then carrying around the keys he'd stolen off her, as calm as if all that stuff was in a play. Total twistoid."

"You got that right," I said. "I'm *really* glad they canceled the play—I've had enough of vampires."

I thought of the book that Philip had given me. The minute I'd gotten home from the hospital, I'd shoved it into the fireplace and stood there crying while it burned. After that I'd felt a lot better.

But I didn't really want to talk about that right then. Frank drank off his coffee, then said, "So how's your family taking it?"

I shrugged. "Predictable. Mom was okay about it, but I could tell she was upset because I hadn't told her everything that was going on, even after I pointed out to her that I didn't know it all myself until it was too late. My dad,"—I took a deep breath—"blamed everything on my mom when she felt she had to call and tell him. How about you?"

"Typical stuff. My little brothers ran a 'why didn't you tell us about the cool vampire kid'—like it was my fault they hadn't gotten to see any blood and guts."

We started trading stories about the idiotic things his younger sibs and my cousins did, laughing and groaning by turns, and after a while I realized that this was the way a friendship gets going. It made me think of Philip again, the silences with the weird music going, and I shivered.

Frank noticed, and stopped talking abruptly.

"Sorry," I said. "I guess I'm going to jump at shadows for a while."

"So jump when you want to," he said, giving me a real smile. Not the sarcastic one he used as armor, but one that crinkled up his eyes and made him suddenly appear a whole lot younger. "Meanwhile, I got this idea."

"What's that?" I said cautiously.

"It's Pilson," he said. "I feel bad for the poor guy,

having the play yanked on him like that. Maybe next year will be better."

"Next year!" I shrieked. "*Never* again!"

Frank laughed, and for the first time in a month, I felt a lightness in my heart.